Everywhere and Nowhere

Joe McCartney

Published by Joe McCartney / Lulu.com

First Printing, 2019

ISBN 978-0-359-56038-7

Acknowledgement

There are so many people who I need to thank. I want to thank my family for all of their help and support throughout this whole process. Mom, Dad, Steph, and Jackie, thank you for your edits that shaped these stories along the way. Jennie Jacoby, thank you for showing me the value of short stories. Chris Holownia, thank you for helping me find my love for writing. Stuart Nadler, thank you for challenging me to push myself and encouraging me to keep creating stories. Ethan Sullivan, without you none of this would have happened. And, thank you to all of my friends who read my pieces during the drafting process. Many of you inspired these characters, so thank you.

Table of Contents

The Graveyard Shift

It had been seven months since mom and I moved from Indiana into my grandpa's home in Woburn, Massachusetts. We lost Dad and my older brother, Ollie, in a car crash coming home from a basketball tournament. Mom and I were supposed to go to those games, but she had been throwing up all that afternoon from a stomach virus. I stayed back to keep her company. I could tell that in some way she felt responsible for their deaths. She always drove to Ollie's games because she got motion sick whenever Dad got behind the wheel. She thought that if she hadn't stayed home, they might not have crashed. I had to keep reminding her that she could barely lift herself out of bed, let alone drive a car.

The 20th of the month paralyzed her, reminding her of the day we lost them, and after several months of sleeping alone in her bed and passing by Ollie's undisturbed room, she took us to Boston. We needed to get away, but we also needed money. Grandpa's bum knee and ruptured left eardrum forced him to retire early, and our moving in over stretched his monthly social security checks. I got a cashier job at Bill & Bob's Roast Beef, a local sandwich restaurant in the town center. The stench of James River Barbeque Sauce and burnt hamburger meat hung on my clothes for hours after my shift. I worked after school and on weekend nights. On Fridays and Saturdays, we stayed open until 2 AM—the graveyard shift. We never had more than thirty people come after midnight. Of the few late-night customers, they were either too drunk to know the difference between credit cards and Charlie cards or too high to decide whether they wanted to order waffle fries or onion rings.

Charlie and Connor Zampatelli became the co-owners of Bill & Bob's after their father retired. Born and raised in Charlestown, they spoke with harsh accents that mangled their r's, so neither of them could pronounce each other's name. Within a couple of months, I became all too familiar with Charlie's gambling problem and Connor's drug habit. Everyone in the restaurant could hear them as they entered the parking lot, blaring Van Halen out of their open car windows. They would come into work, wearing tattered Celtics jerseys instead of their work shirts still reeking of Wild Turkey and Budweiser, howling that Julius Erving "ain't fuckin' shit" or cussing out Robert Parish for missing his free throws and ruining the spread. They also never called people by their real name. Every townie had a nickname, and I was relieved when they found a rotation of pet names for me: "T" and "Fuck Face." At least their accents didn't butcher Fuck Face like when Taylor became "Tayla."

One night while working the graveyard shift, the flow of customers was slower than usual. The Celtics were playing and leading the NBA finals against the Houston Rockets two games to one. I was working the counter next to the radio squawking the game through blown out speakers. I didn't mind the noise. Ollie's prized possession had been a massive poster of Larry Bird featured on the cover of Sports Illustrated, so I liked hearing Bird dominate his competition. Connor was relaying big plays from the food preparation station to Charlie who was filling out that week's checks in the back office. When I asked Connor if he wanted me to move the radio closer to him, he barked back over the clattering of spatulas on the grill, "Hey, Fuck Face, I'll tell ya if I want the fuckin' radio moved. Okay? Make yourself useful and go clean the shitters." I should have known by then to stay out of sight and make myself as invisible as possible.

I returned from cleaning the bathroom at halftime. The Rockets led by one, and Connor was planning to leave early so he could watch the rest of the game at Giovanni's. He and his brother screamed as I tried to take people's orders at the front register.

"Chaz, I'll come back once the game's over! I won't even drink there," Connor pleaded.

"Fat fuckin' chance, booze bag! You don't even have money on this game. Whadya care anyway?"

"It's the fuckin' finals, you bum. You think I don't wanna watch it?"

"If you keep talkin' about leaving that damn grill, I'm gonna come over there and shove that spatula right up your fuckin' ass."

"Alright, alright, Jesus Christ, guy. I won't go to Giovanni's then. Can I at least go to the corner store for some smokes? Is that okay, ya majesty?"

"Fuck off. Get me a pack of Marlboro's while you're there."

Connor left out of the side door, flipping off Charlie. Charlie took over the grill and asked me to move the radio closer to him.

The third quarter began. A short man wearing a black suit entered through the front door. His eyelids hung low on his face, but his stare was intense. Charlie softened the radio. Only the sound of the front door chime and sizzling deep fryers hung in the air. The man took long, calculated steps toward me. After I asked him for his order, he leaned in next to my ear and mumbled, "You give me all the money in that register or you're dead." I thought it was one of the Zampatelli's friends messing around, but then he reached into his jacket pocket and put cold metal against my forehead. With his arm fully extended, he roared, "now!" Charlie rushed over from behind the grill and pushed me away from the gun, knocking me onto the floor. Fear paralyzed me, and suddenly my legs were frozen. Sprawled on the floor, I watched Charlie hold his hands above his head.

"Leave the kid out of this," Charlie begged.

"You owe me a lot of money, Zamp." The man said thrusting the gun into Charlie's chest.

"It's coming. It's coming. Once the C's win tonight I'll be good."

The man looked at me as I pushed against the ice machine to get myself back up on my feet. I kept my hands above my head and my back against the door of the ice maker. He moved the barrel of the gun back and forth between me and Charlie.

"You either give me everything in this register, or you and this punk are dead."

Charlie emptied each slot of the register. He lifted up the dividers to where we hid the hundred dollar bills and gathered them into his hands. He handed over the cash. I imagined the stack must have been close to $1,000. Some of the bills floated to the ground as he fumbled the handoff. The man thumbed through the wad with his free hand, nodding his head up and down as he counted. I caught Charlie's gaze while the man dealt with his loot. He darted his eyes over to the side door then back at me. I couldn't figure out whether he was telling me to run or that he was going to run. Either way, it didn't matter. The man looked up from his cash, pointed his gun, and shot Charlie in the head. Blood splattered onto the support beam behind him, and his body collapsed in front of me.

I screamed. I was searching for words, but only sound came out. The man yanked me by my collar and rammed his gun into my mouth, hitting my teeth. I stopped screaming, felt tears rolling down my cheeks, and tasted hot, smoky metal. An eerily calm expression painted his face as if he had been in this situation before.

"If I was you, I'd stop screaming and tell me where this fat fuck keeps the rest of his money."

The gun in my mouth and fear in my throat choked me. I coughed out desperate breaths over the barrel. I pointed my trembling arm at the walk-in meat freezer in the back. He whipped the gun out of my mouth, knocking into my teeth and sending my skull upwards. I recoiled and thrust my bleeding mouth into my cupped hands. Then, I felt the smack of the butt of the gun into my temple. The impact twisted my body, spraying blood onto the floor and ice machine.

"Now, was that so hard?" he sighed.

He lifted the hinged portion of the counter and walked in front of me. Using the gun to direct, he forced me toward the freezer. Once I got in front of him, he drove the gun into the middle of my spine. I turned the shaky, rusty handle of the freezer, and once inside, a sharp pang chilled my leg. I looked down and saw splattered blood and a dark river going from my crotch down my pants. I was too scared to notice that I pissed myself, and now the dampness was starting to freeze against my leg. I lifted up the box of frozen fries and grabbed the blue bank bag from underneath it. Charlie had thousands of dollars hidden away. He stashed all of the hundred dollar bills in there. He told me that they were good luck at the casinos. I handed the man the bag and watched him unzip it. I nodded vigorously when he asked me if that was all the cash we had.

"Next time, don't make me wait for my money," he said as he slammed the freezer door shut and fastened the lock outside. I began pounding on the door with my bloody fists and screaming for him to let me out. With each cry for help, more blood splashed against the stainless steel. My throat burned as if I had swallowed shards of glass. I jiggled the door handle and threw my entire body into the door. It didn't budge. The damp section of my pants froze into my leg hair. I was out of options.

"I know where Connor keeps his drugs!" I yelled.

The lock to the freezer unlatched, and the door swung open. The man stood in front of the doorway with a sinister smile.

"Would you look at that," he sighed. "It looks like I've got a little helper for the night."

He yanked me out of the freezer by my bloody collar and ordered me to get him the drugs. I hobbled over to the desk in the back office, knowing Connor kept his stash of cocaine in one of the drawers. There were many times throughout night shifts when I'd see him dart over to the drawer, snuff up a key bump's worth of powder, and head back to the grill as if nothing had happened. I felt sleazy abusing this knowledge, giving away his drugs to save my life, but I needed to. This guy was a madman with a gun, and clearly, he was not afraid to use it.

After rifling through the drawers, I found the cloudy baggie of cocaine. I didn't know if it was a lot, let alone enough to keep this guy from jamming me back into the freezer, but he smiled when I handed him the bag.

"The Zamps know how to party, huh?" He asked while bouncing the bag in his hands. Dipping his finger into the powder, he smeared some of the cocaine onto his gums, flashing his gold fang as he exposed his teeth. He shook his head when he finished.

"I'm feeling good, kid! Let's keep this thing rolling!"

Ushering me with the gun, he led me to his car in the back of the parking lot. It was an all-black Mercedes with windows so tinted I couldn't see inside. When I sat down in the front seat, he jammed the gun into my side.

"Don't get any blood on the seat. Use your shirt for Christ's sake."

Holding my shirt up to my aching mouth, I watched as he pulled out of the parking lot and turned onto Main Street.

"Where are we going?" I mumbled.

"I wouldn't be asking any questions if I was you, alright?"

The acceleration of the car forced me into the leather of my seat. The man was whipping around corners and gunning through red lights. Nearly side-swiping parked cars, he continued to ram his fingers into the bag of cocaine and onto his gums. I truly thought I was going to die during that car ride. This coked-out maniac was going to kill me, whether it was by shooting me like he had Charlie or crashing into a telephone pole. All I could think about was my mom and the heartbreak of losing another child to a car crash. It was just she and I tackling the world together, keeping each other sane even though nothing in our lives seemed to make sense any more.

"Slow the fuck down! You're going to get us killed!" I yelled over the roar of the engine.

A maniacal laugh erupted out of him.

"Have a little fun, kid! You're in for the ride of your life, and you want me to slow down!"

When I looked back to the road, I saw us honing in on a telephone pole. At that moment, everything slowed down. This was where I was going to go out just like Ollie by flying through the windshield, splitting my head on the pavement, and bleeding out while the paramedics tried their best. The last thing I remember is the glass from the windshield showering over me. I wouldn't know it at the time, but the Celtics had gone on to win by 3 that night. Charlie didn't have to die.

A few days, dentist visits, and police questionings later, I went back to Bill & Bob's to check in on Connor. The store had been shut down ever since the night that guy killed Charlie, kidnapped me, and crashed us into the telephone pole. He died on impact and somehow, I managed to come away from the crash with only a minor concussion and a few cracked ribs. He was so coked out that he had turned his side of the car into the pole, not mine, saving me after all.

I walked through the door to see Connor with an unkempt beard, shuttling boxes out of the back office. The blood had been cleaned up, but stubborn, streaky stains clung onto the support beam and the ice maker. An open bottle of Jack Daniel's stood on the counter. I didn't see the cap anywhere near it. When I asked Connor if he needed help, he shook his head and pointed toward the paint can in the corner.

"If you could," he paused. "If you could paint over the blood." He choked on the mucus he sniffled back up, wiping away the excess with the back of his hand. "That'd be great, T."

Zugzwang

Sunrays snuck through the gaps between the blinds of their bedroom window and into their Fenway apartment. Flurries of dust shined in the beams of light, swirling in the air like a freshly shaken snow globe. Joe's eyes fluttered as he woke up. He turned to Emilie, still sound asleep, and watched as her chest rose and sank with every snore that slipped out of her gapped mouth. Though neither he nor his wife were moving, it seemed that everything around him was rushing around out of his control. Time raced on, chipping away at the amount of days in Father Time's hourglass. He didn't have trepidations about marrying her when he proposed, yet the despair in his heart felt like someone had dropped an anvil on his chest. The more he looked at his surroundings and the less at his nostalgic, college-aged, puppy love for her, the more he wanted to jump out the window and run as far down Beacon Street as his legs would take him.

*

"I don't know when everything started changing," Joe said as he stared at the ground, refusing to make eye contact with Ben.

"Let's start from the top. Where does all of this begin?"

8

"You want me to go into when I met her or when I stopped being in love with her?"

"Whatever you think will give the full picture."

"Alright, man. She and I met our junior year of college. It was one of those situations where a lot of our friends were abroad and everyone was becoming friends with everyone, you know? So, she and her friends were over my place, and I just couldn't stop looking over at her. I mean, I thought she was one of the prettiest girls I had ever seen, but I had never seen her around campus or anywhere. So, I played it cool. I didn't talk to her or anything that night, but as they were leaving, I saw her and my roommate Matt swapping phone numbers. Right then I thought, 'Fuck me, she's outta the picture.' Thank god Matt had no game and didn't do anything more than that. He could have easily just closed the deal right there. All the kid needed to do was just fuckin' talk to her and bam! I would have been completely out of the game. The shit that bothers me the most about Matt is how he—"

"Let's stay on topic, Joe."

"Alright, alright, my bad. Anyways, so that semester went on, and she and I saw each other at every party or bar or whatever. We'd talk a little bit, but it was nothing serious. I didn't think anything of it, right? She's just another pretty girl I'd never get a shot with. But, one night I got blackout drunk and just started pouring every god damn detail out to her. You remember my Dad's melanoma situation and my buddy Rick that died in the car accident?"

"Of course, I remember. You act like I wasn't your counselor in high school."

"Well, good. You'd be a shit counselor if you forgot," Joe laughed.

"Did you call me up after eleven years to make jokes or to actually get to the bottom of this?"

"Sorry, sorry. Anyways, that's the kind of shit you tell your therapist, not the kind of shit you drunkenly spill to a girl you want to smooch. I guess I told her everything and anything I had to say. Dad getting the melanoma, me having to get some moles removed because the doctor was afraid they were cancerous, Rick dying and fucking me up so bad I thought I had depression when I was just grieving. I forgot all about it, and then the next day, she hit me up and told me that we needed to talk. At that point, I thought that I definitely told her some

9

real, dark shit and couldn't remember which pile of dark shit I shoved in her face. I really didn't wanna do any of that fake 'Let's play therapist' nonsense with her, so I took forever to text back, and I was hoping she would just kinda forget. Nope. She showed up at my door, called me up, and told me that we were going for a walk. So, I was walking with her trying to avoid opening up and was sweating my god damn balls off. It was in the middle of July for fuck's sake."

"How is it still that you haven't changed a bit since high school?"

"What do you mean?"

"You're a grown man now, and you're talking like you did back in my office."

"I'm just upset, alright? Anyways, then we sat down at a bench, and I couldn't even look at her. You remember how I hate eye contact when I'm getting all serious. Everything in me was just pouring out, and I mean everything. I was staring at that reservoir, but I could feel her looking almost through me, seeing every little detail about me. She even almost got me to cry. I had to stop talking for a bit to calm down."

"It's alright to cry."

"Yeah, yeah, I do plenty of that now, don't worry. Anyways, after that day it all sort of came to together, you know? She gave a shit about me, and that was it, really. I waited a bit to tell her that I liked her, asked her on a date, and then bam, we were a couple. I remember how much fun it was to tell people that I liked a girl. It was something to talk about because for some reason everyone gives a shit about hearing who likes who and who's dating so and so. And I had that, that thing that everyone is looking to talk about, and I fucking loved telling every detail of it all. Like, whenever I told girls about the first time we kissed, they thought it was the most adorable shit in the world. I was walking her back to her place after a party, and she kissed me right in the lobby of her building. Completely unannounced, just kissed me. At that point, I was stoked. What a treat to have that just fall in my lap. So, obviously, I keep trying to kiss her, and I had this little plan to kiss her one last time before she got in the elevator. I was gonna do a classic little jump in front of the elevator door to stop it. She got in, the door started closing, I jumped in front of it, and the fucking thing pinned me. The door was crushing me, and I was pretending the thing didn't hurt to act all tough, but man did that shit hurt. She kissed me one last time while the door had me pinned, and then I pushed the thing off of me and went home. I usually tell the story more lovey-dovey than that, but you get the idea. It was just fun to talk about her and us and all the new things going on in our lives. Mom always wanted to hear how Emilie was doing, Dad was starting to pass along his old-timey advice on love, even my brother was supportive of the whole situation, and he's a shitbum who doesn't care about anything.

"How is Patrick these days?"

"Doing fucking awful, but that's for another time. Anyways, after graduation, shit started moving fast. Us moving in together, me proposing to her, actually getting married, I mean, look, I'm 29 years old, and I've been married for three years. That's fucking wild. People are just starting to get engaged now, and I'm way past the finish line. The thing is, once you get married, nobody really gives a shit about your wife or stories about your wife or any of that. Wives are boring. It's like, 'yeah, yeah, yeah, we get it, you love her, next thing.' And to be honest, that's when I started getting bored too. Look, Ben, I was just trying to feel good, you know? Feel something, anything. I was just so damn bored. I felt like I was locked in a cage or something, and that's when the whole gambling problem I told you about on the phone came alive. I had always bet on games and stuff, but never more than like twenty bucks at a time. Before I knew it, I was throwing hundreds, thousands on literally anything. I was wasted at 2 AM one night when I had told Emilie I had a work thing and would be outta town. I was bombed in some random motel, and I threw five thousand dollars on a Russian basketball game I couldn't even watch. I just kept watching the tickers move, and slowly my team started to lose, but I felt fucking nothing. I should have been pissed or something, but nope. It was just another bet, another loss, kinda as if nothing had happened at all. I remember in college when I'd scream over a ten-dollar loss or lose my shit if I won twenty bucks, but, it just felt hollow. And you wanna know the worst part of it all? I was down in Chinatown late, real late one night. I ended up in some shady-ass basement of a store with a bunch of guys gambling on Russian roulette. They were all screaming in Chinese, I couldn't understand shit, but these guys were throwing some serious cash down on the table. This guy had the gun in his mouth. He had sweat pouring down his face, and he was looking around at everyone with these big bug eyes. He clenched down on the barrel and screamed his head off like he was amputating his leg or something. Then just a little click. He lived, people were cheering and shit, and that's when I pushed my way through these guys to the table. I sat down, threw ten grand in front of me, and held out my hand for the gun. These people were silent at that point. I mean, it made sense. Some random shmuck comes in off the street and willingly sits down at a Russian roulette table? That shit doesn't happen too often. So, I spun the barrel, held it up to my temple, and then that little click came out. I doubled my money that quick. But, Ben, I was bored. Bored playing Russian roulette. You know how fucked up that is? I mean, that was the only time I did it, but how fucked is that?"

"Joe, you've got a serious problem you need to take care of."

"You don't think I know that, Ben? From the outside, nothing should be wrong. Sure, Emilie is great and all, but it's just not exciting anymore. I don't get all excited to see her like I used to. I remember when I would be counting the days to the weekend when we first started dating because it meant I could see her and could sleep in the same bed as her. Now, she's just become such a staple in my life that it just doesn't hold the same weight anymore. I don't know what to do, Ben. I really don't.

"Well, you have to make a move."

"What do you mean?"

"You ever play chess?"

"Yeah, but what does that have to do with anything?"

"There are times in chess where you'd be better off not moving any of your pieces, because if you were to move one, you'd put yourself in a more vulnerable position. If you could, you'd make a null move, if you've ever heard of the term. You'd defer your turn and let the other player go, but as you know, that's not how chess works. That's also not how life works. You can't keep yourself in the same position because you're scared of what's going to happen next. You need to make a move, Joe. I don't know what the move is, but the place that you're in right now is in no way, shape, or form the right place for you. I know you're probably scared to admit it, but you might have gotten it wrong with Emilie. Being 'bored' of your wife this early in the game is a bad sign."

"So, you're saying I should call it off."

"I'm saying you need to make that call for yourself."

"That's the thing, Ben. I can't make that call for myself. I know I'm going to keep putting this off, hoping that one day Emilie is going to make the move for me. I almost wish that she realizes that she doesn't love me or something anymore. That way I can pretend it blindsided me. I could tell my parents and friends and everyone else that she thought things weren't working out. I don't want to have to admit I fucked up, or admit to her that I need something more from her. This isn't her fault—she's a great girl. It's me. I'm the fuckup who has been chasing and chasing after shit. And I know that she loves me, she tells me all the time, and it's starting to hurt to see her fully committed to this shit when I'm just going through the motions. I don't want to be the idiot who got married too early, Ben. Every one of my stupid buddies kept saying how I was jumping head first into this, and my stubborn ass didn't believe them. Now here I am whining to my old guidance counselor, too fuckin' scared to talk to his own wife. Ben, you gotta tell me what my move is here."

"Talk to her, Joe. Talk to her."

*

He rose from the bed and walked into the bathroom. He craned his head underneath the faucet, cupping his hand and lapping water into his mouth. The icy-cold water stung his hand, yet almost tasted sweet on account of his dehydration after a night out of drinking. The floor boards creaked as he tiptoed back into the bedroom. From the doorway, he looked at Emilie still sound asleep on her side of the bed. She probably wouldn't notice if he turned right around and booked it toward the door. She'd still be snoring away as he darted around Kenmore looking to hop on the first train he could take. He could ride it all the way to Park Street and then South Station, get a bus ticket to New York, and hide out with his old college buddies. Maybe he could even take a flight down to Florida, rent a piece of shit apartment, and go completely off of the grid. He had gambled his way into financing this apartment, how hard could it be to do again? Florida definitely had poker rooms and sportsbooks. All he'd have to do was find the right people, the right ins, and he'd be all set to fully vanish from the world. If he disappeared, everyone else would have to do the work for him, make moves on his behalf. Sure, it wouldn't be the same as faking his own death, but total disappearance had to be the next best thing.

But he did none of that. He crawled back into bed with a throbbing headache, lingering regret, and immobilizing guilt that were weighing heavy on his shoulders. Emilie woke up as he tucked himself back under the covers. She nestled her head into the nook of his neck and shoulder, wrapping her arms around his chest. As she ran her

13

fingers along his arm, she whispered, "I wish we could just stay here all day."

The Little Star

Michael Hennessey knelt down to be eye level with his son. Tyler's gaze wouldn't leave the ground. He was focused on counting the cracks in the pavement of the parking lot. Michael placed his hands on his son's slight shoulders. Tyler stopped counting.

"If you get scared, remember what Ms. Abby told you to do. We'll be in and out quick, okay?"

Tyler nodded in agreement. They grabbed each other's hands and headed toward the doors of the Essex Mall. This would be his first trip into a place like this.

The doors of the Essex Mall opened, revealing the large, hectic ecosystem that hid behind the neutral-colored, exterior walls. Harsh fluorescent lights and potent perfumes bombarded Michael. Tyler hadn't noticed the commotion yet. He was too preoccupied repeatedly circling his index finger over his thumb. They continued through the entrance, passing by more neon signs, snippets of conversations, and waves of white noise.

Kiosks stood every twenty feet, each displaying their own brand of meaningless trinkets, knock-off clothing, or fad trends. They all squeaked different music from small, blown-out speakers, trying to get any and all attention they could. The anxiety inside Michael started to clog his throat. He felt Tyler beginning to pause for longer and longer at each display they passed. By the fourth kiosk, Michael was leading his son through a minefield of frivolous objects, subtly ushering him to move forward. The store was a few hundred feet away, but Michael knew all too well an eruption was imminent. Hushed whimpers and sharp breaths escaped Tyler, and a tight squeeze of his hand followed with each sound.

"It's okay, buddy. Dad's here."

Tyler didn't look up at him. His eyes darted around at the myriad of distractions. Sounds, sights, and smells came in too many forms, and now, after bringing his son here, Michael realized the sheer number of potential triggers.

The tremors in Tyler's hand became noticeable. The fear that camped in Michael's throat transferred to his son, as if their hand-holding could provide more than just guidance and firm pressure. In an all-too-familiar shaky tone, Tyler recited the order of the solar system. His pace quickened. Strollers creaked—Mercury—feet shuffled, illuminated signs flashed bright—Venus, Earth—clocks ticked in syncopation, coins clanged on the ground, bags crumpled—Mars, Jupiter, Saturn—lines on the floor passed by too quickly to count—Uranus, Neptune—Tyler let go of him, collapsed to the ground, and shrieked—Pluto.

A crowd formed an enclosing circle around Michael as Tyler wailed and screamed on the ground. He scrambled to calm Tyler down. His pleas couldn't sneak around Tyler's hands shielding his ears. Tyler squirmed as Michael placed his hand on his son's back, trying to apply firm pressure like Ms. Abby had said Tyler found comforting. He knew the people thought he was raising a monster he couldn't control. They couldn't know this wasn't an ordinary tantrum. He didn't yell, he didn't punish, he didn't do anything wrong. He just wanted to see if this trip could happen. Not today, he guessed, and maybe not ever. Throwing all the guidance and clinical teachings to the side, Michael lifted his son off of the ground and into his arms. Tyler's soon-to-be seven-year-old body fought back, squirming and wriggling to escape. Michael took off with his son. He needed to get him away, somewhere safe, anywhere but here.

*

16

Nearly four years ago, inside Washburn & Stanley Pediatric Center, Michael was searching for the right questions to ask the graying doctor. Tyler sat on the observation table, playing with the Velcro on his shoes. In Michael's hands, the puzzle piece logo on the pamphlet looked like a gymnast doing a full split. The doctor continued talking, his voice reverberating in the air. Michael's eyes alternated between the pamphlet and his toddler son. "He can still live out a normal life." *Normal*. This word hung heavy, hovering over him. He didn't want to believe that something was wrong. Tyler's life had barely even begun, and now, there was something *abnormal* about him. Raising Tyler singlehandedly was already difficult enough. He needed a lifeboat, not another anchor chained to his foot.

"Autism is a manageable neurological disorder, Mr. Hennessey. All it means is that you and your wife are going to have to take different sorts of precautions when it comes to Tyler." He looked at his left hand and rubbed his thumb over the groove of where his wedding ring used to be. The tan line it left was becoming less distinguishable. He didn't want to bring it up. He nodded along with the doctor, letting his version of the world still have her exist, wishing he could live in it too.

"I can refer you and Tyler to a great therapist. Her name is Abby Mantinolli. All of my patients have had great success with her." The doctor scribbled down a number on the back of a business card and handed it to Michael. Between the pamphlet and the business card, he had all the resources needed to get his three-year-old the proper care. He just wished he had someone else to help him along the way. There wasn't an instruction booklet for raising a child, for being a good father, and that's what scared Michael the most.

*

Back at their cramped apartment, Tyler clung onto his favorite rocket ship blanket, still shaken up from the incident at the mall. Michael sat across from his son's bed, hoping his multiple apologies meant something. Silence floated around in the room like a satellite orbiting in deep space. Finally, Tyler mumbled, "I hate that place." This was the first thing he said in over an hour.

"Me too, Tyler. And don't worry, you'll never have to go back there again. I promise." He hoped Tyler would react or speak, just something to let him know that this incident would blow over, and everything was going to be okay. And hopefully, by some miracle, he wished Tyler wasn't mad at him.

Tyler finally fell asleep. Michael left the room and walked into his own. He lifted the sheet off of his desk to reveal an unfinished model of the solar system. He got back to work, carefully painting and shaping the different planets and moons. He needed to get every detail correct. Details were important. Everything needed to be exactly as it should be.

A "happy birthday" table cloth covered the kitchen table. The dimly illuminated apartment welcomed the sparse decorations. The duo just finished eating their mac and cheese and peas dinner, Tyler's favorite meal. Tyler had a blank look about him, as if he didn't quite realize they were celebrating, let alone that today was his birthday. Michael wondered if he was still upset about what happened at the mall. He desperately hoped the waiting surprise would make up for his mistake.

After cleaning the table, Michael told Tyler that there was something for him. They walked into Michael's room. The sheet was covering the now complete model. Tyler looked around, not really knowing where the present could be hiding.

"Go lift up the sheet, bud. That's your present." He walked over to the sheet and slowly unveiled his gift. The clog found its way back into Michael's throat.

Order, precision, specifics: these were things Tyler liked. The solar system embodied all of those qualities. Every planet followed its own orbit, circling the sun in a steady rhythm and path. There was a solidified structure to the solar system, aside from Pluto crossing into Neptune's orbit every 248 years. But even Pluto's obstruction of order had order in itself, sticking to its consistent schedule of 248 years. Order rules in outer space, even among the seemingly infinite stars, comets, and asteroids.

Tyler stared at the model. Colored Styrofoam perfectly mimicked the size and ratio of each planet. Every detail found its way into the model, from the tilt of Neptune's ring to Mars' two moons. A "wow" exploded out of Tyler. He turned toward his father and rammed into him to hug him. Tyler didn't like touching—he rarely even let Michael hold his hand. Now, Michael embraced his son, remembering to hold him tight because of Ms. Abby's firm pressure advice. He looked down at his son, whose smile was even bigger than his own.

"Tyler, this is the first time that you've hugged me."

"Oh. Okay."

A Horrible Little Shop

Hidden in the suburbs of Boston, tucked away between shops and stores, sat a peculiar little flower shop with a man and his plant, and no, not any plant, but a plant the likes the world had never seen. The man, a man known to many as the hunchbacked man with the thinning black hair and dark rimmed glasses, was truly an odd, odd man. Ever since he was a boy, back when people still knew him as Claudio Von Claude, he had a fascination with bugs and worms and plants and trees. Cast away by his peers, and hardly ever watched over by his parents, Claudio spent nearly all of his time in the woods alone with his creatures, his crawlies, and his green, leafy friends.

As time went on, what once was his fascination turned into a full-fledged obsession. Countless encyclopedias and hundreds of volumes later, Claudio had more knowledge of plants than he knew what to do with. The ordinary bored him, having no more time for regularly blooming Giant Hogweeds or warm colored Dodders. So, he began to cross-breed and mix all sorts of plants like Angel's Trumpets and Titan Arums and other marvelous specimens to create some truly extraordinary combinations. He converted his home into a laboratory, a lab full of lamps and fans and watering rigs so complex and elaborate even he lost track of where all the pipes and wires came from. Between his lab and hand built green house, he opened a shop to display all of his beautiful little creations, which had everyone in town flocking in to witness with their very own eyes. If it weren't for his stature and gangly, crooked smile, people would have stayed and shopped for a while. But none of that mattered to Claudio, for he cared more about tending to his plants than connecting with people.

Of all of his creations, one plant stayed hidden from the public eye. His favorite of all plants, of all of nature for that matter, was the Venus Flytrap. Those hairs that looked like teeth, lobes that became a digestive stomach capable of making acids and enzymes, were just some of the qualities that Claudio prized. He began making his own rare breed, wishing for something grand. He worked late into the night, grinding and whittling away to create the perfect sight. Then finally, a truly peculiar flytrap arose, no taller than a pencil and with a bud no larger than his big toe, budding teeny, tiny, razor-sharp teeth and lobes of a brooding, deep purple. When he poked his finger into the lobe for the first time, the flytrap snapped its jowls shut and drew some of his blood. The flytrap savored the blood while Claudio held his finger in pain. After bandaging himself up, he noticed the plant wiggled and shimmied as if it were trying to speak. He bent down to the plant, bringing his face quite close, and asked in his clumsy, awkward tone what it wanted. Miraculously the plant hummed, like that of a whimpering, hungry dog.

"My plant, my plant, my sweet, sweet plant. Are you a hungry, hungry plant?"

The plant opened its jaws, revealing its purple trap and shiny spikes. Taking that sign as a yes, he dug his grimy fingers into the soil beneath a towering Viper's Bowstring Hemp. Rummaging through the dirt, throwing clumps onto the floor, he finally found a plump little worm wriggling between his fingers. He ripped it in half, catching the falling guts with a cupped hand, and he walked over to his hungry, hungry flytrap. He dumped the sludge from his hand into the flytrap's mouth along with the rest of the worm, and with harsh snap, the plant clamped. It squirmed with joy, purring as it ate, pulsating its little lobes as it devoured the worm in its mouth.

"Marvelous, marvelous, my little friend! Keep chewing, keep growing! I'm going to make you the mightiest flytrap of them all!"

In no less than two weeks, the plant grew about three times its size, looking more like a desk lamp than a plant. The blades in its mouth sharpened to that of ten doctors' scalpels, the brooding purple coloring its cheeks grew darker around the edges resembling rubble after a fire, and its stem thickened and turned pliable, allowing the not so little plant to twist and turn its unbecoming head. And by this time, no, the plant was no longer just a plant, because it had a name which Claudio had given. Vincent the Venus was born, still hidden in the back room of the store. But with Vincent becoming increasingly large, its appetite quickly followed suit. No longer would little worms and tiny flies solely satiate. Its palette desired real, authentic food, not that which could be found in the soil or in a spider's web. When Claudio dumped an entire supply of bait and tackle worms into Vincent's mouth, it chomped and it turned until the bait was all gone. Then opened its mouth up again with a whimper and a cry, flashing its gut-stained, razor-sharp teeth.

"Are you still hungry, Young Vincent? How could this be?"

Vincent mewled in a pathetic cry, begging Claudio for more food, just something, anything to satisfy. Looking to his refrigerator, Claudio reached for the door and grabbed his wrapped deli cuts. Roast beef, still bloody, that's how Claudio liked it, practically still mooing when he bought it.

"I'll give you this—this is all I have, Sweet Vincent. Now eat, eat!"

As the blood dripped off of the wax paper and into Vincent's mouth, it squirmed with anticipation. Each drop sent a twang through its stem, bending and kinking out of excitement. Claudio released the roast beef into its mouth, careful as to not lose a finger or hand, and watched as Vincent devoured the meat. As if it were chewing, it adjusted its lobes while the meat sat in its mouth, shifting and resetting the hinges of its two petals. Claudio put his hands around the plant's head, rubbing and caressing the beast while it dissolved the fresh meat with acids and enzymes.

"Who takes care of you, Little Vincent?" he cooed. "I'll always take care of you, my carnivorous friend."

With Vincent's budding new appetite, Claudio became a frequent customer at the butcher shop. Rather than cold cuts and deli meats, he brought home slaughtered pigs whole, hunks and chunks of meat, and even the buckets of slop the shop owners were throwing away. Keeping time precisely, he fed his creation three times a day, and with each meal came a squeal that warmed Claudio's heart. Vincent was growing day by day, sprouting new leaves along its stem, which was looking more and more like a stalk or a trunk. But all of this feeding was getting expensive, and the men at the butcher shop were growing quite concerned over the man who wanted the carnage and guts and bones of a day's work. One of the butchers even caught Claudio stalking around the dumpster behind the store as he was reaching his hands into the heap of discarded animal remains. He scurried away when the butcher yelled at him, leaving empty handed and concerned about how he was going to feed Vincent that night.

As he approached the shop without any dinner for Vincent, deeply worried about letting down his friend and afraid of hearing him whimper and cry all night long with a grumbling tummy, the neighborhood tabby cat was perched in front of his door. Nobody in the entire strip of shops and stores knew who the fat, orange tabby cat belonged to, yet everyone would leave bowls of water and food for the sluggish feline. It would make its rounds to each of the stores, dipping its husky frame into each bowl of treats, and then plop itself in front of one of the entrances. Claudio crept toward the tabby cat while it groomed itself licking its paw.

"Hello, little kitty, hello, hello."

He lifted the cat and pulled it into his arms, petting and stroking its orange fur.

"Who's a good little kitty cat?" He prattled. "It's you. It's you. It's you."

With the cat in his arms, he entered his shop, chiming the front bell as the door swung open. Walking through the maze of flowers, petals, and plants, he led himself and the tabby cat to the back room where Vincent was waiting. Vincent had gotten so large by this point it no longer sat on Claudio's desk, no, rather it sat on the floor, upgrading from its tiny ceramic holder to a giant terracotta pot that looked more like a witch's cauldron. What once were the baby teeth in its mouth had developed into rows of shredders like that of a shark, and when its jaws were fully open, it could easily fit an extraordinary watermelon in its jowls.

"Oh, my Resting Vincent, I have a surprise for you."

Vincent perked its head up from its slumber. It had a habit of coiling its gargantuan stem into its pot and resting its head on the bed of soil beneath it while Claudio was away or after devouring a full meal.

"How would you like a taste of this?"

He held the tabby cat over Vincent's mouth, yet Vincent didn't open up right away. It was used to bloody things, things that smelled like food, things that were as dead as wilting roses in a bouquet.

"C'mon now, I know you're hungry my Dear, Dear Vincent."

The plant opened its jaws, and at the sight of his truly terrifying teeth, Claudio flung the tabby cat into its mouth. Vincent fastened its mouth like a bear trap, crunching and snapping the bones of the cat so audibly it echoed throughout the back room. The tabby cat let out a blood curdling shriek, one so high and so shrill it managed to escape the thick walls of Vincent's mouth barely being muffled at all. With its incredible frame, Vincent began chewing like a ravenous piranha, blood spilling out of the corners of its mouth and trickling into its pot and staining its soil.

"Yes! Yes, My Vincent! You love it, don't you?" Claudio squealed.

Vincent kept chomping and crunching on the poor tabby cat as Claudio fidgeted with flutters in his heart. His beast was truly marvelous, nothing like that which the world had ever seen, but he knew the public would never understand, never quite comprehend, what made Vincent fantastical. They would see it as a behemoth from hell rather than a spectacle of science and creation. They'd want it dead, and not just dead, but with its head cut off, stem chopped in two, ripped from the comfort of its pot, and buried miles beneath the vast, vast Earth. He vowed to never let that happen, to never let anyone or anything harm his work, his friend, his Vincent. Once it was done chewing, Vincent spat out the tabby cat's tail, mangled and wetted down from the acids. It coiled its stem back into its pot, sighed a purr of a full belly, and set its head down in the blood-soaked soil for a nap.

Almost a month went by with Claudio following the same routine of feeding Vincent. Finding stray cats and dogs, scavenging up slop from the butcher shop, his life became about procuring enough food for the rapidly growing Flytrap. But with all of his time and attention directed to Vincent, the rest of his creations in the shop began to suffer. The Wolfsbanes in the corner lost their purple hue. The Witch Hazels curled into themselves like a shriveled-up mess, barely recognizable to their original, healthy state. Even the Dracula Orchids started to crumple and fold, drying up like someone had left them in the baking, hot sun. Fewer and fewer customers came into the store, yet Claudio barely noticed. Even when the shop was open, he constantly shuttled in and out of the back room to check on Vincent. He loved to just watch it rest and marvel at its size. Spilling out from its pot, it sprouted a series of leafy, hairy vines from its stem that now had the thickness of a fireplace log. Its head had grown to the size of an over-inflated beach ball, allowing Claudio to place whole stray dogs, like Collies, German Shepherds, and Labrador Retrievers, into the plant with ease. But food was growing scarce since Claudio singlehandedly had wiped out the entire population of stray animals and nearly all of his earnings from the shop.

One night while Claudio was closing the shop, haphazardly watering the crumpling, crinkling plants, he heard a wail from the back room. He had only fed Vincent twice that day, praying it wouldn't notice going without dinner, but alas, Vincent's stomach kept a regular schedule. He hurried to the back room and saw Vincent writhing around in pain. Flailing its vines, whipping its head, it bellowed out shrieks and screams looking for Claudio to remedy its gluttonous hunger.

"My Vincent, please! I'm ever so sorry! I'll go to the store first thing in the morning, I promise, my Hungry, Hungry Vincent."

His apology and promise didn't appease the beast, for it only howled louder and thrashed its massive frame around in its pot, spilling the soil beneath it onto the ground.

"What do you want me to do, Voracious Vincent? I can't just get a plump piggy all willy-nilly!"

The whimpers from Vincent deepened into a churning growl. Baring its chompers in a sinister flare, its teeth now aligned like the blades of an industrial wood chipper. It faced Claudio expecting an answer.

"I've given you everything and anything! What more could I give you! I want to feed you, I really, really do, Insatiable Vincent!"

His creation was upset, his other plants were wilting away into the soil, and he had nowhere to turn. All of his hard work would be in vain if Vincent withered away to nothing, but there was no food in sight, no cold cuts in the fridge, no animals to ravage. Everything was in shambles. Then he looked down at the scar on his finger, the scar Young Vincent left on the first day of their encounter. Sticking out his arm, he held it out by Vincent's mouth while looking the other way.

"Here, My Starving Vincent, here! Take my body and chew me up! I can't let you go!"

Its growls muffled into confusion. It fell silent with its mouth closed.

"Just do it already! Bite it off and eat!"

The beast shook its head, rejecting the offer to eat its maker. Claudio was growing more frustrated by the minute. If he couldn't feed it, and couldn't feed himself to it, he felt that there was just no option to question.

"Damn it, Stubborn Vincent! Do as I say!"

With his temper at a raging high, it ignited the anger back in Vincent's body. It twisted to Claudio, grumbling a brooding sound, fanning its assortment of teeth like the train of a peacock, and looking ready to bite. Claudio threw himself at Vincent with rage in his eyes, clutching his fists ready to strike, yet Vincent snapped first, engulfing Claudio's body in one bite. It chomped and chewed and crunched and gnawed on Claudio's body until it became a thick, bloody paste. Once it was done slaughtering its owner, it spat out the dark rimmed glasses, broken and chipped like they had been shoved in a blender.

Yet, now with Claudio gone, nobody was there to feed Hungry Vincent. The shop stayed locked, and the customers stayed clear and far away from the gruesome display of crumpled, shriveled up flowers. Nobody would ever know there was a pool of blood beneath a man-sized Flytrap in the back room. There was no more life in the shop, only Vincent remained.

After its typical post-meal nap, Vincent awoke with its creator nowhere in sight. It turned and twisted its head, looking for the hunchbacked man, yet never found poor Claudio anywhere in the back room. It was getting hungry, surely it was time to eat, but remorse and regret were starting to fill its body. It wailed and whimpered hoping for Claudio to appear by its side, and as time passed, its howls intensified. Vincent was starving and morose, surely Claudio would walk in at any moment.

But that time never came. Vincent curled up into its pot. Its vines became brittle and short. The teeth in its mouth began to fall

26

out. The purple of its lobes faded to black. Vincent let out one last, sad, defeated whimper, remembering what it had done to Claudio and wishing it could spit him back out and reunite with its only friend. And the shattered dark rimmed glasses sat nearby on the floor, watching Old Vincent crumple and wither away.

I Dreamed of Diamonds

To play for the Boston Celtics, let alone just play in the NBA, has always been my dream. Ever since my dad nailed up a backboard on top of the garage in our home in Burlington, Massachusetts, basketball has been my whole life. I'd spend hours after school putting up jump shot after layup. When brutal Boston winters came and blanketed the entire driveway in a foot of snow, I would shovel it all off and practice my free throws in layers of bulky coats my mom forced me to wear. My parents raised me to be tough, play hard, and to "never take shit from anyone." The summer after eighth grade, I was playing basketball on the courts outside of the high school. The high schoolers arrived and forced me off the court, cutting in front of me on the next game. When I finally got in, the massive starting center for the team intentionally clotheslined me as I went up for a shot. Bleeding on the ground, I remembered my dad telling me that the bully only wins if you don't fight back. I got up and swung for his temple and knocked his ass onto the pavement. Sure, all of his buddies kicked the shit out of me that day, but after that, nobody ever tried to scrap with me. Never take shit from anyone.

I was fortunate enough to earn a basketball scholarship to Belmont Hill School, a private school my parents couldn't have afforded otherwise. I led the team, no longer just a team of rich, white kids, to its first undefeated season and Independent School League Championship. That same year, I received an offer to Boston College. I played there for four tough years, slowly climbing my way from bench warmer to one of the best point guards in the ACC. Then, finally, on the day of the NBA draft, the Celtics used their last pick late in the second round on me. On that day, I did it—I had made it.

During my first game, with my entire family in the stands, we were giving the Orlando Magic a beat down. Up twenty points in the fourth quarter, I blew out my ACL while going up for a rebound. I hit the floor so hard it felt like my brain was rattling inside my head. Crumpled and agonizing on the floor, I couldn't move my right leg without it feeling like someone was stabbing me. The athletic trainer rushed over to me. He struggled as he tried to lift me onto my feet. My fists ached from punching the hardwood in frustration. I knew it would be a long time before I played again. When I saw my mom standing upright in the bleachers with her hands covering her mouth and with tears welling up in her eyes, it made the situation real. I was fucked.

My injury sidelined me for the rest of the year. By the time I came back, I was sent down to the G-League team, the Maine Red Claws. When I heard the news, my throat fell into my stomach. I watched my dream wither and then slip away from me when it had been so close just months before. It felt like God had stabbed a rusty knife right through my heart.

Out of this entire experience, the most devastating aspect was the competition. The teams were a bunch of guys like me, young and hungry looking to break into the NBA. If a guy wasn't young, he was washed-up and had been floating between Showtime and the empty stands of G-League games. Richie was the Red Claws' veteran, a scrappy, white shooting guard nearing his late twenties. Richie had been bounced from team to team countless times, but his off-the-court behavior kept him from making it big. Strip clubs, girls, drugs—these were the things keeping Richie from the spotlight, but it didn't seem to bother him. We'd come back to the locker room after getting blown out, and he'd have this nonchalant walk about him, shrugging off the loss like it was nothing. He was already focused on where he was going to party later that night. After about a month of keeping to myself, hustling in the gym and grinding in the weight room, I noticed that Richie recognized my potential. Whether he was trying to mentor me or just hoping he could ride in the wake of my success, he clung to me. Sure, I liked the guy, but I was dedicated to get back to where I had been rather than partying at every chance I could get.

There was one night in particular when I got wrapped up in what we called "Richie Bullshit." We had just beaten the South Bay Lakers and were about thrity minutes from downtown LA. Richie came up to me in the locker room, looking like he was already coked out of his balding head.

"Yo, X, we gotta hit up the strip club tonight," he said as he was thumbing through his phone, looking for girls or dealers.

"C'mon, Richie, you know I'm not into that."

"When are you gonna live a little, man? We're in Los Fucking Angeles. You mean to tell me you're gonna just go back to the hotel and do nothing."

When I nodded my head, a look of disappointment took over his face. He physically wiped the disgust off with his hands. A loud grunt escaped between his fingers.

"X, it's just a strip club, man. One night out isn't gonna keep you from getting called up to the C's."

He had a point, though vague and misleading. It wasn't like this was going to keep me from getting back onto the Celtic's roster. Guys did this sort of stuff after games—I knew that, but the thought of strip clubs weirded me out. I never understood why a group of guys would want to stare at the same naked chick while they're all in the same room. That never seemed like fun to me, but I couldn't be the guy to say no and have to explain that I would rather watch TV until I passed out than throw money at a girl with fake tits.

"Fine, Richie. But I'm not staying out that late, man. We've got another game tomorrow."

"Fuck yeah, X!" He yelled as he yanked me into his arms. "Xavier Wilkins and Richie Mason hitting the town!"

Later that night, Richie and I, along with a few other guys from the team, pulled up to Velvet Gentlemen's Club. Richie had decked himself out in a flashy watch, a shiny blazer, and wildly lavish sunglasses even though we would be in a dark, neon lit room. He led our crew right up to the bouncer, greeting him with an emphatic handshake.

"My man!" Richie hollered. He was oddly comfortable at these kinds of places. He probably had gone to any club he could find after games during his brief stint with the Los Angeles Lakers. He told me he had always wanted to come here but never got around to it. The Lakers had traded him after he was caught drunk driving at 4 AM.

Once we got inside Velvet, all of my initial thoughts about strip clubs were right. It was my first time ever in a place like this, but I still knew this definitely wasn't the place for me. The whole place reeked of tequila and perfume. They kept the lights so low that I could barely see my teammates who were standing right next to me. Everything was blanketed in a red and pink hue from the neon fixtures rigged on the walls. The girls were overly friendly, brushing a hand on our chests and whispering sweet nothings into our ears as they strolled along through the crowd. They clearly knew we played ball—a crowd of seven 6'6" dudes was a dead giveaway. They knew these guys threw cash around. Richie had withdrawn one thousand dollars before coming here. Some of the larger bills peeked out of the back pocket of his designer jeans. I was hoping my teammates wouldn't notice that I only brought $50 in singles. Nearly all of my paychecks went right into the bank. Money was tight growing up, and my parents taught me to save every penny I made. Even with five zeros trailing behind the number in my bank account, I was still cheap, thinking about the times when kids at Belmont Hill would make fun of me for wearing the same blazer and tie to school every day.

The girls sat us down on suede couches by center stage. Within seconds, a flock of girls approached us, asking if any of us wanted a lap dance.

"Yo, blondie!" Richie hollered at one of the prettier girls, pointing right at her nearly exposed chest. "Give my man X a dance. And don't be shy." He slipped a fifty-dollar bill into her black lace bra, clearly taking his time to grope her. The rest of the guys were cheering him on as he worked the wadded-up bill into her bra. My anxiety about the lap dance had me shifting in my seat. I felt my palms dampen, my ears heat up, and my left leg bounce uncontrollably. As the girl mounted me, all of my muscles stiffened as if they were replaced with rocks. She guided my clammy hands onto her waist and ass, and I awkwardly retreated them onto the legs of my pants.

"Aww, someone's a little shy," she whispered into my ear, taking time to bite my earlobe. "How about we go into the back room away from all these people?"

I needed a way out. There was no chance I was going to go back there with her, even if everyone wanted the new guy on the team to do it. I squirmed out from under her, mumbling about how I needed to go to the bathroom.

"Don't be such a pussy, X!" Richie yelled as I stumbled away, knocking into chairs and couches. I hurried to the bar that was out of sight. As I waited for the bartender to serve me, one of the strippers floated up next to me. She wore less makeup than the other girls, yet her lips were perfectly outlined with cherry red, a stark contrast from her porcelain skin. The tip of her nose carried a slight hook. She was stunning.

"Must be your first time here," she said while reaching over the bar and grabbing two bottles of Bud Light. "I've never seen someone run from a lap dance like that before. You might need one of these if you're gonna enjoy yourself here." She handed me one of bottles and brought the other to her lips. She tucked the loose strands of golden hair behind her ear like she was drawing curtains. She introduced herself as Diamonds.

Diamonds and I talked at the bar for nearly two hours before I realized all of my teammates had left the club. It wasn't until Richie came up behind me, patted me on the back, and told me he was heading out that I found myself truly alone with her. The locks of her blonde hair fell from behind her shoulder and in front of her face, somewhat shielding her mascara-outlined, emerald eyes.

"You wanna get out of here? We've got a room in the back we can go to," Diamonds murmured, darting her eyes toward the back of the club.

"Diamonds, I don't know if that's such a good idea."

"Call me Megan, alright? It's after hours now."

At that point, she wasn't a worker anymore. Her flirtatious attitude was genuine. She didn't want me because I played basketball, or because I had money, but because there was a serious connection between us. In a way we were both misfits, looking to belong to something else. She shared her aspirations of becoming a nurse and that she was working at Velvet to pay her way through school. I told her that I just wanted to get back on the Celtics roster, play in The Garden again, and get the hell out of Portland, Maine.

When we walked into the back room, time melted into a puddle. I couldn't tell whether we had sex for a minute or for hours. Maybe it was because of the drinks, but I felt like we were in a different world altogether. She and I had been drifting into our own universe, floating together in endless space. I've had girlfriends in the past, girls I had told I loved them, but none compared to this.

I held her in my arms afterwards, caressing the small of her back with my hand. Her head nestled in the crook of my neck, hair sprawled out over me like a wave spreading itself onto the rocky Portland shore. The pungent perfume that lingered on the furniture along with the lilac of her hair crept into my nose. Our breathing aligned, inhaling and exhaling in unison. I wanted to say something, but that would have disturbed this moment—a moment I wanted to encapsulate and keep for cold, rainy Maine days. She lifted her head, brushing her hair out of her face and behind her shoulders. I couldn't help but peek down at her exposed chest. She got up from the bed, put her clothes back on, and told me that she'd be right back. As I was putting on my pants, jingling my belt buckle, I could have sworn I heard her mutter "I'm sorry" under her breath as she left the room, but I'd never know for sure. I wanted to think that she cared—I really did, but I would never find out.

By the time I was fully dressed, a thunderous thump echoed through the room. A man in a black leather jacket and a semi-undone button down shirt that exposed the ringlets of his black chest hair kicked in the door to the back room. He must have been about six inches shorter than I was and losing almost all of his hair. He flicked on the lights, blinding me. When my vision cleared, I noticed the tire iron clenched in his fist.

"Hey, hotshot!" He roared. "You think you can sleep with the girls? Huh!" He flung the tire iron into the wall cracking the plaster. I held my hands up by my head, screaming at him to calm down.

"She came on to me, man! I can explain!"

"I don't give a shit what happened. You don't get to fuck the talent! I'm not running a god damn brothel at my strip club!"

"She took me back here!"

"I don't give a shit what you've got to say, Wilt Fuckin' Chamberlain. You don't get to fuck my girls!"

I figured that he must have been the owner of the joint. I probably could have kicked his bald, doughy ass, but he had a weapon and clearly was ready to shatter my skull. I was losing control of my breathing, hyper-ventilating between my apologies and attempts to explain the situation.

"Just get Megan back in here! She can explain all of this."

"Who the fuck is Megan, and why the fuck should I listen to what you've gotta say?"

At that point, three bouncers walked into the room and stood behind the guy with the tire iron. The biggest one of the bunch stepped in front of the other two, cracking his knuckles like he was about to square up in an MMA fight. All hope of kicking the shit out of the fatass owner vanished. I was fucked, and he could definitely tell that I was starting to realize just how screwed I was. I kept searching for words, anything to try to get me out of this situation, but nothing was coming out. All I could do was stand in front of him, nearly pissing my pants, praying that Megan would walk through the door and save the day. I wouldn't know it at the time, but that moment would never come.

"Look, guy, I don't give a fuck what you gotta say to me. I really fuckin' don't," he said while smacking the tire iron around in his hands. "You either cough up five grand, or I break both of your knee caps. Got it?"

"I'm not paying you five thousand dollars," I spat back.

"Oh, you wanna get tough now, huh? You really wanna fuckin' do this?"

One of the bouncers rushed toward me. He pinned my arms behind my head. I struggled to move, and, as I did, he jammed his fist into my back. My knees buckled underneath me. As I opened my eyes, I saw the man launch his fist into my stomach. He knocked all the air out of my lungs, and a sound escaped me as if there was a ghost trapped inside of my body. I collapsed to the floor, toiling to breathe.

"I'm gonna put it to you real simple, here. I'm leaving this room with five thousand bucks. It's up to you whether you wanna walk tomorrow."

He tapped the tire iron on my right leg, finding the exact spot of my scar.

"I know all about you, kid. I know your whole story. I saw you play college ball, and I heard about your little ACL injury. It'd be a real shame to see you blow out that knee again. We'd hate to see that, wouldn't we boys."

His goons laughed with him. It felt just like it did in middle school when those high schoolers ganged up on me with that asshole of a center. I couldn't fight back this time. I couldn't tell this guy to go fuck himself or swing at his chubby fucking face. At that moment, I was so close to getting back to Boston, back to The Garden, and back on the roster. I couldn't let all that just slip away, but I wasn't going to let this asshole shove me around. My dad's voice echoed in my head that I shouldn't let people fuck with me, but the roar of the crowd at TD Garden made it that much harder to hear him.

"What's it gonna be, Xavier? You giving me my money or you leaving this place in a wheelchair?"

*

The following year, I was sitting on the bench for the Memphis Grizzlies as we were playing the Los Angeles Clippers at LA. I made it out of Maine and back onto the Celtic's roster only to get traded at the deadline. I was getting fewer minutes in Memphis than I was in Boston. Barely playing and losing almost all of our games, I was frustrated. It seemed like I was running in circles trying to get back to where I had been before my injury.

After we lost that game, one of the rookies asked if anyone wanted to go to Velvet. I walked over to him and whispered to him, "Stay the hell away from there, and if you do decide to go, stay the fuck away from Diamonds."

The Comedian

John waited back stage sipping on a half empty water bottle as the opening act finished up her set. He couldn't tell whether his nerves or the condensation from the water bottle made his hands so damp. Somehow the anxiety that came from awaiting crowds always managed to buckle his knees and accelerate his breathing. Four years of perfecting the same routine never quite felt like enough. His delivery could have been sharper, his charisma more inviting— everything could have been improved.

After the emcee announced his name, John walked onto the stage. The heat from the overhead lights hung over the hardwood. Droplets of sweat from his back and chest soaked into his black t-shirt. The roar from the crowd exploded and then muffled into a swell of sound. The audience was transformed into brooding silhouettes, illuminated by the spotlights of phone cameras and screens. Reaching the microphone stand in the center, he waved to the Capitol Theatre.

"Thank you! Thank you! Who knew so many complete strangers would come out to see me when my father won't even come to one of my shows?" He waited for the crowd to take the bait, riding on that high of having the audience think a joke is over. Those small, hushed laughs where strong streams of hot air rush out of nostrils were mere key bumps, knowing that the set up already had them going.

"It's fine, though, I think if a dead guy were in the audience a lot of people would be freaked the fuck out." Half laughter, half verbal recoil. "It's fine that I make that joke because he was a total fucking asshole." He punctuates his punch line by taking a sip of his water, relishing in the crowd's boisterous laughter.

*

Three and a half years ago, John and his parents were seated for dinner. The sound of clinking silverware onto worn porcelain plates cut through the bitter Boston air, wafting with the stale scent of the Marlboro Gold dangling from the corner his father's mouth. With every one of his father's audible puffs of smoke, John searched his mother's face for a hint of disapproval. She kept her eyes down at her plate. His father had worn her down after years of arguing about his smoking habit, and by that point, there was almost always a cigarette in his mouth. There were times he had an extinguished butt nestled between his lips, sucking and chewing on the filter. The green, soot-stained ashtray on the corner of the table hadn't been emptied in weeks. Crumpled, spit-shriveled butts formed a sluggish mound of orange like a leaf pile by the storm drain after a downpour.

"I got an opener slot at the Laugh House for this weekend," John broke the silence. "It's paying one hundred for a set."

His mom picked her glance up from her meal. A coy smile snuck onto her face.

"That's great, Johnny. Things are really starting to pick up for you."

His father wheezed a raspy cough, beginning one of his familiar coughing fits. John could almost feel the tar and sludge that lined his father's throat with every laborious heave of his chest. Through it all, he continued to cut away at his food, eyes locked on the plate in front of him.

"You hear that, Dad? I got a gig for the weekend."

Barely lifting his bloodshot, glazed eyes from his meal, only bringing them halfway to John's chest, he mumbled his words. They were almost unrecognizable.

"Yeah, yeah, I heard you. Good job."

His passiveness echoed throughout the kitchen. John knew that his father didn't care—he had stopped giving a shit years ago.

"That's it? Just a 'good job?' That's really all you have to say to me?"

"Yeah, Johnny. That's about it," he said after an exasperated sigh escaped his mouth. "Way to go."

"How about we change the subject?" His mom asked. She looked around at John and her husband. No amount of redirecting was going to extinguish the fuse his father's blatant apathy had just ignited nor smother John's impending explosion.

"Can't you even pretend to give a shit about me?"

"Johnathan, that's enough. He's being supportive," his mother dismissed.

"No, he's not, Mom. He's just nodding along hoping I'll shut up. Isn't that right, Dad?"

"Look, Johnny, we've been down this road enough now. Can't we just eat the dinner your mother cooked for us in peace?"

"Not until you actually mean what you say, you asshole."

"Johnathan, I will not have that kind of language in my house, and I will not stand by and let you talk to your father like that." She clenched her fists and tightened her lips, falling into a stern, flat line across her face.

"Stop talking to me like I'm a god damn child, Mom."

His father plucked the cigarette out of his mouth and smooshed it into the ashtray. Its embers sizzled on the dampness of the pile.

"Johnny, look, I'll let you be disrespectful to me all you want, but your mother is where I draw the line."

"Disrespectful? Where the hell do you get off calling me disrespectful when you don't even try to give a fuck about me?"

"Johnathan, Franklin, that's enough. Stop it, both of you," his mother snapped.

His father reached for the pack and Zippo nestled in his front pocket. In a fluid, all-too-familiar motion, he snagged a cigarette with his teeth and brought a flickering flame to its end.

"Because, Johnny, I just don't care what you do anymore," his lips curled around the new cigarette, muffling his words. "I really don't. Nothing you do really changes anything. So, good job on the thing. I hope it all works out in the end, but really, I just don't care," he exhaled a puff of smoke toward John.

"You two animals have ruined my night long enough." Her chair screeched from underneath her as she stood up. She threw the napkin from her lap into her meal and stormed off onto the back porch.

"All your mother wanted was a nice dinner. Look what you had to do."

"Look what I did? This was all your fault, asshole."

His father closed his eyes and pinched the bridge of his nose, turning the edges of his fingers a yellowish white from the sheer power of his grip. With a breath in, followed by a series of deep, wheezing, mucus-filled coughs, his eyes met John's. The indifference in his voice subdued to a mere whisper.

"It's not my fault. None of this is my fault, and you know why? This was all you, Johnny. I never told you what you should or could do with your life, and maybe that's where I went wrong. But, hey, you know what? Go pursue your comedy and see what the hell I care. Maybe I'll see you on SNL. Wouldn't that be something?"

"Fuck you, Dad. You're a god damn deadbeat," John hissed.

His father took a long drag of smoke before taking hold of the cigarette. With it between his pointer and middle finger, he rocketed a punch at John's mouth. Blood spattered over the kitchen floor. John felt his lip scorch where the ember met his skin. He collapsed, smacking the linoleum with the side of his skull. The overhead light casted a shadow that masked his father's indifference. Looking up, with his hands cupped over his face, his eyelids fluttered as he writhed on the floor.

"Clean up this mess when you're done."

He threw his cigarette on top of the overfilled ashtray and walked out of the kitchen to the back porch.

*

"Anyone else recently single in the crowd tonight?" High pitched enthusiasm echoed through the theater.

"Yeah, I had to cut it off with my girlfriend a few weeks ago. She was bat shit crazy. She would always love to role-play: she would be herself, and she would want me to be literally anyone else."

*

It had been one year since John moved out of his parent's home and nearly six months since he last spoke to his mother. Frank had been shoveling the driveway and collapsed face first into the snow.

The doctors believed that his COPD led to the heart attack that took his life. John only heard that much about his father's death because he hung up on his mother when she asked him if he would be attending the funeral. Part of him wanted to go and curse everyone out for being there, for cherishing his father's life. The animosity in John's heart toward Frank became a blinding rage, but his overwhelming apathy ultimately kept him from going. John would never realize how similar he and Frank actually were, sharing a stifling indifference to life.

John sat on the couch of their sparsely decorated apartment as the television flickered late night ads. The front door slammed louder than usual. His girlfriend, Mary, had gone out drinking again after work and must have misjudged how hard she needed to throw the door behind her. He turned around to her unevenly stepping in, clopping her salt-stained boots like a limping horse. She headed toward the kitchen, ignoring John's questions about her day. He followed behind, rushing to the fridge to grab her a bottle of water and the plate of dinner he had made a few hours before.

"Look, it's been a long day for me," she huffed as she plopped herself into a seat at the kitchen table. "Just go to bed. I'll be right there."

Placing the food and water on the table, he grabbed the chair next to her. When he tried to hold her hand, she slithered it back into her coat pocket.

"What're you doing?" she sighed.

"What do you mean? I wanted to hold your hand."

"John, c'mon now. Just go to bed."

He had noticed the growing emotional distance between them, but up until that point, it was ignorable. Their conversations had grown shorter and more infrequent, and they rarely had sex anymore. John had become infuriatingly impotent. He fully believed he loved her and that she was the love of his life. She was the woman who understood all of his intricacies, yet anytime they got remotely physical, blood refused to go to the right areas. He'd hide afterwards, trying to see if he could get anything going by himself. Problems continued to pile on top of each other just like shoveling snow in a storm, when every gust of wind fills in the areas that were just cleared, forcing John to reclaim the plot he had just finished.

"Is there something we need to talk about?" John pleaded, holding his hand out in case she experienced a quick change of heart.

"No, John. Go to bed. I'm fine."

"It just seems like—"

"It's alright, John."

"Can we just—"

"For fuck's sake give it a rest!" she snapped.

He had been taping together their relationship for so long he didn't notice all the cracks spreading out like a spider's web. A breaking sheet of glass can only be handled so much before it shatters completely, cutting and leaving shards in the hands that work to repair it.

"I'm sorry," he grumbled. "I'm just trying to be a good boyfriend."

"Look, John, I know you're not going to want to hear this, but it's time. We both know this isn't working. It stopped a long time ago, and I know that you felt it when it stopped working too. Sure, we had a lot of fun at the beginning, don't get me wrong. But I have to move on with my life."

"I can't say I'm all that surprised by this," John exhaled.

"Yeah, and I've been fucking Henry for a while now. I'm pretty sure you even knew. It's not like I was hiding it all that well. I was with him earlier tonight."

John had noticed her smelling of perfume after nights out. He noticed the spring in her step as she walked around the apartment, probably after the times she saw Henry. There were little dark marks along her neck and collarbone he didn't give her. She just looked happy. He could tell she was falling in love, but he kept pretending she was falling for him all over again.

As he sat there defeated, Mary waited with her hands held to the sky as if to say "what now?"

"So, where do we go from here?" John asked.

"For starters, it'd probably be best if you moved out."

"But, I have nowhere to go."

"I know, but you've had time to figure that out. We both know deep down you were trying to hold this together so you had a place to live. Don't even act like I'm making that part up."

His head hung in his cradling hands.

"I'm going to sleep at Julia's tonight. I'm sorry, John. Best of luck with everything. I hope it all works out."

*

"But enough of my shitty life, let's get to the fun stuff. You know when you're watching Netflix and it asks you 'Hey, are you still watching?' That's gotta be the most annoying thing in the world. Imagine if other parts of your day did that. Like if your dinner said, 'Hey, are you still eating?' or if your life asked you, 'Hey, are you *still* trying?'"

*

John moved out of Mary's apartment within a week. He took what little stuff he had and the little bit of money he had saved up from shifts at the diner and drove his beat up, rusting-at-the-edges Camry to New York. A small apartment in Williamsburg became his new home. Former tenants etched their names into the wooden door frame as if to prove they survived living in 1C—Marisa E., Griffin B., Kat G., and other names which were too worn out to decipher. The light of a rattling ceiling fan solely illuminated the apartment void of any natural light.

John had been watching Netflix on his computer and scrolling through Instagram waiting for an open mic night. Since most clubs didn't open until midnight, John slowly became accustomed to living nocturnally. Sleeping through most of the day, John saw few people and even less sunlight. A photo of Mary and Henry appeared on his feed. They had gone skating at Frog Pond. Her gloved hand rested on top of his chest as she lovingly smiled toward him. He scrutinized every detail the photo gave him: the Christmas lights in the background, the color of their beanies, the way her laughter seemed forced as if she were flaunting her happiness to the world like a peacock expanding its train. He had been staring at the photo so long he didn't realize his show had stopped—"Are you still watching?"

The fan above him creaked, oscillating its light ever so slightly. He threw his phone onto his bed and climbed up on the chair to yank at the base of the fixture. It seemed sturdy. The base had been anchored with five sturdy bolts. The metal felt cool and strong in his hands. The splotchy floor board loomed underneath him. He hopped down off of the chair and listened to the restored silence that echoed off of the walls.

John walked over to the tattered Nike box underneath his bed and grabbed his baggie of loose Xanax. He had made plenty of jokes about his Xanax dependency and abusive habits while on stage. Alcohol super charged them, he'd say. As his drug habit evolved into a

42

full-fledged addiction, people told him that Xanax was dangerous. If he were to accidentally drink too much or have one too many Xanax bars, he'd end up dead in a coffin, but that warning never got through to him. John would always answer that if someone took thirty Advil it would be the last headache they'd ever have. All drugs were dangerous, some more than others, but John didn't seem to care.

A few Xanax bars, a half bottle of Jack Daniels, and a half hour wandering the streets later, John found himself in a cheap motel room with a prostitute. He was fading in and out of consciousness, feeling as if all of him was floating to the top of his head. The familiar weightlessness of Xanax flooded him. Hours blurred into moments. Words slurred into sounds. The prostitute was growing exhausted of John tugging at himself on the other side of the bed.

"Look, kid, I don't care if that thing doesn't get hard or not, but I'm leavin' here with my money," she said. Her Brooklyn accent blanketed her words.

"Five minutes. Just, just more five minutes," he mumbled.

"You're not makin' any sense. How fucked up are you? You need me to get you help or somethin'?"

"No, no, I just five minutes. I got it. Five."

"I'm outta here. I'm not havin' some kid die on me. I'm fuckin' gone."

She got up and rummaged through his pants next to the bed. He didn't even notice her going through his wallet. She snatched close to fifty dollars and slammed the door on her way out. By the time John had the briefest moment of sobriety, the woman had been gone for almost half an hour. Nothing was working right. No comedy clubs wanted him, he had isolated himself from everyone back in Boston, and his impotency still reared itself at the worst times. All of the pent-up frustration broke free. He threw the television at the wall, shattering the screen into hundreds of pieces. The drawers of the dresser snapped and splintered after John yanked them out. The shards of glass and slivers of wood that penetrated his skin drew blood. He was a naked, bleeding mess, destroying everything in sight. Once the Xanax and booze kicked back in, he collapsed onto the floor among his wreckage. He wouldn't wake up until the sunrays crept through the blinds and into the motel room. The pings of pain were scattered along his body, covering his arms and hands. He was sober enough to notice the destruction he caused. Shame and regret washed over him in an all too familiar way. All he could think about was his father's raspy, coughing voice: "clean this mess up when you're done on the floor."

*

"That's all for me. Thank you, New York, for coming out tonight! You were all fantastic!"

Later that night after the show, John stood outside alone. People exiting the theater congratulated him for his show, and in return, he gave a meek wave. Nobody stayed to talk. Everyone had places to be. The sounds of traffic and dim street lights were his company as he smoked his cigarettes. Every time he removed the filter from his lips, he grazed over the scar his father left him. A little twitch of angst jolted through his body each time.

Just as he finished his last smoke, stomping it into the sidewalk and releasing a puff of smoke, his mother approached him from the exit. He felt his face turn pale, feeling all the blood leave his head and surge into his beating chest. She rushed at him and smacked him with her purse.

"How dare you disgrace your father like that on stage," she scolded. "I can't believe you would have the audacity to say that after all the shit you've put us through? You know how many people asked me about you at the funeral? How humiliating it was to have to lie to everyone because you were too petty to go? He's your damn father, John. Have some respect."

"Respect? You seriously want me to respect him after what he did?"

"Oh, I'm sorry, was he the one that went radio silent on everyone in his family?" She was practically screaming at this point, drawing the attention of passersby. "Was he the one that left his mother in the dark? Was he the one that made everything about him? No, Johnathan, that was you. You've been so caught up in yourself that you never looked around at what was going on. Sure, he wasn't the best father, but he tried, god damn it."

"Well he did a shit job at trying!"

"Any worse than you, John? Huh! I only knew to come here because Aunt Phyllis called me up last week after she saw an ad in the paper. I had an idea of the kinds of things you were going to talk about, but I was more horrified than I thought I could be. He wasn't the bad guy, John. You were. I hope you somehow are okay living with yourself after all this."

She stormed off, leaving John alone once again. He looked up at the sign above the theater and watched the flashing lights twinkle around his name. That sinking despair in his stomach didn't disappear like he thought it would. He made it, or so he thought.

Queens

Before visiting Provincetown in the summer of 1988, Daniel McLoughlin couldn't have named a single gay person in all of South Boston. As far as he knew, everyone, whether they were his classmates at South Boston High School or the patrons during his shift at Broadway's Best Pizza, was straight. If someone was even slightly flamboyant, everyone within earshot would berate him, calling him a fruit, fairy, or faggot. Almost always, those sorts of altercations quickly escalated into a full-blown brawl that inevitably sent someone to the hospital with a bashed face and busted ribs.

Nearly one year ago during one of his night shifts after a Bruins game, two of his friends, Paul and Jack, came in for a slice. Throughout the game, they had been sipping cheap vodka from full flasks hidden underneath their jerseys. By the time they got to the pizza shop, they were absolutely trashed. They stumbled up to the counter, screamed their order at Daniel, and sat down in a booth. They were shouting as they talked, making Daniel constantly twist his head around toward his boss's office to see if he was coming.

"You fuckin' boneheads gotta calm down," Daniel whispered to them as he handed them their pizza. "I'm trying to not get fucked again because of you two."

"Oh, shut the fuck up, Pizza Bitch," Jack laughed.

They continued to shout from their booth. Paul and Jack were best friends, and it certainly showed. They laughed at all of each other's stupid jokes and would wrap their arms around each other during their laughing fits. Their drunkenness only added to their displays of affection, throwing their bodies back as they heaved with laughter. After five minutes of their hollering, two guys stood up from a nearby table.

"You two fuckin' homos need to take your dicks out of your asses and shut the fuck up!" One of the men barked.

"The fuck you say to me, you fat piece of shit!" Paul cried back.

"You callin' us faggots, dumpy motherfucker?" Jack snarled.

Within moments, Daniels' friends and the two guys were throwing haymakers at each other's heads. The crash of tables, along with the screams of onlookers in the restaurant, pierced through the air. Daniel jumped over the counter and tried to hold Paul back. As he was holding his friend, one of the guys sucker punched Daniel in the temple. He felt his body collapse to the floor, smacking his shoulder into the linoleum. The split at his brow was gushing blood onto the floor. The entire restaurant cleared out before the cops came and arrested both his friends and the two guys. Daniel spent the night in the hospital with a concussion and had to get four stitches above his eyebrow. Needless to say, Daniel didn't consider being homosexual as an option. People were straight, and if they weren't they got the shit kicked out of them.

Though he was great at playing pretend, dating his girlfriend, Isabell, for over two years and talking about other girls' asses around his friends, his performance as a straight guy muddied his identity. He had shoved and stowed away any remotely gay thought into the deepest chasm of his mind. The lies he was telling himself began to take the shape of truth. Those guilty feelings from his gut started to dull, letting him tell Isabell he loved her without some shame in his heart. He had even convinced himself he paid more attention to Jennifer Grey instead of Patrick Swayze when he watched *Dirty Dancing*.

On July 13th, 1988, Daniel lied to his parents and Isabell. He told Isabell he was away with his family and told his parents he was with Isabell at her cousin's wedding in New Hampshire. He was unaccounted for. Hidden behind his ruse, he bought a ticket for the Fast Ferry out of Boston Harbor to Provincetown, the gay capital of America. The rumors of P-town lured him. He had heard of the rainbow flags hanging in front of houses, how men walked down Commercial Street holding hands, and of the cross dressers and drag queens parading in boas and miniskirts. Sure, he wanted to witness for himself what total and utter freedom looked like, but he needed to navigate through his locked away feelings. They needed to be experienced and proven either true or false. It was time, having been eighteen for almost six months at that point, to address his elephant in the room.

As he plopped down in a corner booth on the ferry, he began flipping through the pamphlet of P-town that was on the table. He couldn't tell if the shifting in his stomach was from the waves smacking into the boat or his nerves tugging at his intestines. The ferry slowly filled up with more passengers, coming through the entrance like an assembly line. Once they were through the door of the ferry and hidden from the eyes of Boston, the masks started to come off. Daniel noticed men holding hands and how some would drape their arms around another man's shoulders. Halfway through the trip, two men pecked each other. What most likely was commonplace for them smacked Daniel as if he ran into a brick wall. Nobody glared. Nobody hurled insults. Nobody got up and started a fight like he had seen so many times at his late-night shifts at Broadway's Best. All hostility, the familiar hostility and blind anger that brewed in what seemed like everyone from South Boston, evaporated into the warm, sea-soaked air.

As the ferry pulled into the Provincetown Harbor, the sun was descending into the ocean. Swirls of purple and orange clouds speckled the skyline. The familiar stench of greasy, fried food snuck into his nostrils, only this time the brine from the ocean accented it better than the pang of Menthol Newports. Passengers standing on the bow of the ferry were waving to the crowd gathered at the pier. Onlookers were hollering at the boat. Some were honking loud, brass horns incessantly, cheering for the passengers as they walked along the platform from the boat to the dock. It was as if they exited reality as they entered into the realm of P-town. Daniel remained silent as he passed the tan, shouting men wearing neon tank tops, exposing their sculpted shoulders and pecs. Many of the guys were in better shape than the people he boxed against at Peter Welch's Gym. Though Daniel knew a lot of the onlookers could probably take him, there wasn't that floating suspicion, that impending fear of a fight or a brawl. These people weren't itching to scrap, and that only added to how unsettling it all was.

Daniel followed the pack of passengers down the pier and to Commercial Street, the main road of P-town. Shops and restaurants lined the street, yet there was no consistency of what business was next to another. The stores he passed were too different. Everything wasn't just a pizza place, corner store, or bar like in Boston. A psychic palm reader popup was nestled between a kid-friendly puzzle store and a sex toy emporium. A hippie clothing shop that had marijuana incense burning just outside the door faced the two candy shops across the street. While Daniel was walking down Commercial Street, flocks of drag queens approached him. They wore stark velvets, shimmering rhinestones, and frilly lace. Mascara, foundation, and blush blanketed their faces. They looked like nothing he had ever seen, and they blurted sexual innuendos as they handed out flyers for their shows.

"Hey, sweet thang, you look a little young, but I won't tell if you won't."

"Come to the cabaret tonight, and if you do, that won't be the only thing coming tonight."

"Look at Mister Muscles over here. He could beat me up and off, isn't that right, ladies?"

Nothing made sense here, but he was slowly becoming more comfortable wading in the unknown of P-town. This was what normal looked like around here. Of all the flyers he was given, the one for the *Drag Queen Talent Show of a Lifetime* at The Crown and Anchor caught his attention. The model on the front, a queen posing in the likeness of the Morton Salt girl, complete with umbrella and spilling canister, appeared as if she was directly looking at Daniel. She was enticing him to come watch, and he hesitantly made his way to The Crown and Anchor. Going alone made him nervous. His stomach felt like a washing machine with a brick tumbling around inside. Yet, he fought through his nerves. He rationalized that nobody would judge him here, that he could sit alone at the bar and just observe, and that he could always slip out the back door once the show got started. If things got too weird, he could escape.

Ever since his junior year of high school, Daniel had been using a copy of his older brother's license. Many mistook them for twins growing up, and if it weren't for the fading scar above his eyebrow from one year ago, they would still be nearly impossible to tell apart. At least the scar made him look tougher.

The bouncer at The Crown and Anchor barely looked at his ID. Once he saw that he was from Massachusetts and heard his Boston accent reveal itself in the few words they exchanged, he waved him right in. Daniel walked into the club and through the aisle of chairs facing the stage. He hopped up onto one of the barstools and ordered a Budweiser. When Daniel went to hand the bartender cash, he waved him off.

"On the house. You look like you need to unwind."

By the time the talent show began, The Crown and Anchor was inundated with people, spilling out of the exits and back onto the street. The room was damp with sweat and vodka lingering in the air. The emcee emerged from behind the curtains, wearing only a sheer apron. He wasn't hiding anything, standing with his legs apart clearly to showcase himself. The crowd hollered and cheered as he paraded around the stage, announcing the talent for the night. One by one, fully dolled-up drag queens strutted onto the stage. Imitation celebrities, like Cher and Madonna, followed behind the queens in intricate, fluffy dresses and wigs. Each queen would wave or blow kisses to the crowd, and with each gesture, the entire audience roared. Even the bartender who had been serving Daniel let out the occasional "woo" when some of the queens came out. But, just like with the shops, there was no order, no rules, no normal to these acts. The last performer to walk on the stage was a 10-year-old boy with a saxophone. He was wearing a Red Sox hat and a crisp, tuxedo t-shirt. This was just a normal kid, standing on stage with grown men wearing dresses and makeup. Daniel leaned closer to the bartender.

"Is this place always like this?" Daniel yelled over the roar of the crowd.

"I've never seen a kid on stage, but other than that, I'd say so. You want another drink?"

With each performance, the cogs in Daniel's mind churned. These queens were grown men, pretending to be celebrities or loud, brassy women. In some ways, they were almost parodying being a woman. Yet, at that moment, they *were* these women. To the members of the audience, and even the queens themselves, it was as if Cher and Madonna really were performing at The Crown and Anchor. They sounded like them, looked like them to some degree, and everyone was playing right along with it. These queens were redrawing the line between make-believe and reality. How could something be and yet not be at the same time? When did playing pretend become real?

The kid with the saxophone was the last act to perform. He squeaked out *Take Me Out to The Ballgame*, bopping his body along with the notes of the song. Once the crowd recognized what he was playing, they all sang along in a deep, drunken harmony. People began wrapping their arms around one another, swaying their bodies to the flow of the music as if they were listening to a ballad at a rock concert. The people at the bar next to Daniel held their beer bottles in the sky like they were lighters and waved them in the air. The older man in front of Daniel, a man with a meticulously trimmed beard and a thin, partially-open white button down, spilled some of his beer onto Daniel's leg. He apologized, wheezing with his cigarette stained, raspy voice, and tried to dab off the beer with a wad of napkins. Daniel swatted away his hands like he was trying to kill a mosquito.

"It's fine. It's fine," Daniel dismissed.

"Well, alright then. Last time I help you out," he hissed back.

The emcee herded all of the acts back onto the stage. He was eliminating contestants that didn't get enough applause. The saxophone kid, Cher, and Madonna were the last three acts standing. The deafening wave of sound coming from the crowd was like rolling thunder. Cher went on to win the competition. The emcee handed her an over-the-top trophy and placed a tiara on her head. Daniel snuck out of the back door and onto the outside deck as everyone applauded. He hoped that it looked like he just needed to have a smoke.

Daniel leaned his entire weight onto the wooden guard rail overlooking the bay of Provincetown. The Christmas lights hugging the rail reflected off his glasses and illuminated the condensation on his beer bottle. The man in the white button-down shirt walked up to him. Daniel almost didn't notice. He was too focused on looking out to the water and wondering if anyone in Boston had seen him board the ferry that brought him here.

"I'm sorry about earlier with the whole spilling thing," he sighed, rolling his eyes as he talked. "I can be a bit of an ass sometimes. Especially when I've been drinking. You know how it goes."

"It's alright. I'll take your word for it."

The man struggled to light his cigarette. The salty winds kept blowing out the flame.

"I take it you've got a boyfriend by the way you swatted my hand away," he said with the cigarette still tucked between his lips.

"Girlfriend, actually. Her name's Isabell," Daniel muttered.

"And she's okay with you coming to a drag show? Look, you don't need to let me down easy. I've been rejected hundreds of times before you were even born," he condescended. The flame finally caught the end of his cigarette, blackening the edges of the paper. He took a long drag and exhaled a large cloud in Daniel's direction, but the wind carried it away toward the ocean.

"No, I'm serious."

"Oh, you're one of those?"

"One of what?"

"Those guys that have girlfriends or wives and pretend to not be gay but do the kind of stuff you're doing right now."

"Woah, I'm not doing anything right now," Daniel snapped back.

"No need to get all testy. Jeez, I guess it must be pretty stuffy in the closet, huh?"

"Oh, fuck you. I don't need this kind of shit."

"Alright there, Mr. Boston, let's calm down. I'll stop making jokes if you'll stop looking like you're going to throw me into the ocean."

"It's really hard to when you have that damn smirk on your face."

"Okay then, answer this for me. Why did you come all the way out to P-town and go to this drag show?"

The man raised his eyebrows as he waited for a response from Daniel.

"I wanted to see what this place was like, alright?"

"Is that really all you wanted to do, Mr. Boston? Just come out here to walk up and down the street and catch a show? Or did you want to see what it was like to not have to hide behind that big strong guy act?"

Daniel broke his gaze from the ocean and turned his body to the man.

"I was like you once too, kid. I put up that same little charade of being all tough and pushing every emotion I had to the side. Sure, I wasn't as ripped as you are, but I definitely buried all feelings I had that would have gotten me kicked out of the house," he coughed as he took another long drag, almost burning a quarter of the cigarette down in one inhale. "All I'm saying is that while you're here, drop the game. Nobody is judging you here. We all play for the same team here."

Daniel hung his head, refusing to look the man in the eye any longer. The man finished his cigarette, releasing his final puff of gray smoke to the wind. He flicked the butt into the sand beyond the deck.

"If you ever decide to come back and want a real look into this place, my name is Colin." He patted Daniel's shoulders as he left the deck. Daniel slowly turned around to watch him walk back into The Crown and Anchor. The door swung open, slowly oscillating until the view of the bar inside disappeared.

On the ferry back to Boston, Daniel kept checking his watch. His Sunday shift was starting in a few hours. The snake-like veins in his forearms protruded more than usual. He thought about the drag queens. That world was something so foreign, so abnormal, and yet somehow all clicked together perfectly. They all liked playing pretend, becoming the characters they envisioned themselves to be. They got to perform like real musicians and celebrities. Daniel wondered when Colin had decided to drop his act and start living in the make-believe.

Everywhere and Nowhere

It had been almost nine months since Olivia died, leaving David widowed to raise their fourteen-year-old daughter, Michaela, by himself. Olivia was driving home on New Year's Eve, 1998, when a drunk driver crashed into her at the intersection of Adams and Hancock Street in front of the Seven-Eleven and Atlas Liquors. The driver was a seventeen-year-old barely off of his Junior Operator License. He was transporting a pack of three other drunken kids to a party and fled the scene only to crash head on into a telephone pole just a few blocks away. The drunk teenage driver and his trashed friends died on impact, while Olivia struggled to survive as the jaws of life pried at the crumpled mess of metal that was once a car door. She was pronounced dead at the hospital three hours later.

Olivia's funeral, which was gruelingly painful for David, having to comfort his grieving child while managing his own despair, was rather peculiar. Olivia's brother delivered a sentimental, polished eulogy that brought nearly everyone in the church to tears, and David's niece sang an immaculate rendition of *Ave Maria* similar to that of a weeping angel, but grief and sadness soon turned bizarre.

On the night of Olivia's funeral, long after Michaela had gone to bed, David discovered that he could appear in any location instantly. He sat alone in the basement flipping through photo albums. He came across a picture of Olivia standing on top of the dunes of Long Nook Beach in Truro, Cape Cod—the place he proposed to her twenty years before. Sitting in a creaky wooden chair, he reminisced about that day, remembering how the sand cradled his knees and how the susurrus of the wind played with Olivia's wavy brown hair. He closed his eyes, taking a long, drawn-out breath. As he inhaled, he recognized the salty breeze creeping into his nostrils. He opened his eyes to find himself standing at the peak of Long Nook's dune, staring out into the endless ocean. He crouched to the ground and picked up a handful of sand. As he released his grip, he watched the grains fall, clinging onto the wind and flurrying toward his feet. Standing on Long Nook beach that January night certainly wasn't a stress-induced dream, rather something fantastical. He was hearing the whispering weeds and sea grass that lined the dunes and catching wafts of the briny, ocean water. Everything was exactly as he remembered it, perfectly picturesque with waves rhythmically crashing onto the shore, spreading water across the sand like the strokes of a painter's brush. David was certainly there at Long Nook that night.

He thought of his home in Quincy, of the creaky chair he was in moments ago holding the photo album, and in an instant, he appeared back in the chair. It was as if he was never gone, yet sand still speckled the edges of his black dress shoes. He thought of other places, imagining himself at the Boston Common where he and Olivia had their first date, and he inconceivably appeared next to Frog Pond. He began rifling through his memories, and with each new location he found himself standing in a new setting. His vision of beaches, sidewalks, and homes melted and blurred together, like the blades of a spinning ceiling fan cycling so fast that the paths of the blades form an entirely new figure. The landscapes around him changed to match his memories. After appearing in different locations, David pictured himself back in his basement, photo album of Olivia in hand, and just as before, he flashed back into his home.

*

David and Michaela were approaching Thayer Academy. Michaela sat silently in the passenger seat of the car. In the weeks prior, Michaela refused the idea of leaving her hometown friends and

Quincy public schools to attend a stuffy, snobby private school out in Braintree. She and David argued daily about whether she would attend Thayer. They didn't have the money for tuition, nor did Michaela have all the credentials to actually be admitted on her merits, but she was a faculty's child. David was approaching his twelfth year as a teacher and fourth year as the head of the math department. The admissions office was unsurprisingly more accommodating for children of faculty, and Thayer generously discounted faculty tuition by ninety percent. Thayer was a golden opportunity, David explained to her, but all she could think about was leaving her friends and feeling like an outsider. Eventually Michaela conceded, rather unwillingly, succumbing to her dad's dream for her.

As David turned into the main entrance of the campus, he softened the radio and asked how she was feeling.

"I'm fine," she answered dismissively. He glanced over at her. She was still staring out of her window. With the radio muted, the silence echoed through the car. As he began to turn the car into the teacher's parking lot, Michaela mumbled, "Could you let me out here? I don't want to walk in from the teacher's lot."

"Sure, I get it. Too cool to be seen with me, huh?" The corners of his mouth curled as a stream of air escaped his nostrils. Michaela looked unamused, her eyebrows resting flat across her forehead. Jokes would have to wait a while, he thought. He pulled the car over to the sidewalk next to the Glover Building.

"Alright then. Head right into Main, and Mrs. Lyons will tell you where to go. I'll wait for you at the Math Office at the end of the day."

As she was exiting the car, she turned back around to face David: "The other freshmen will be there? I'm not going to stick out as a faculty kid?"

"All the other freshmen will be there. I won't blow your cover. Good luck. You're going to be fine. I love you."

She darted her eyes at the passing car on the left before looking at David and murmuring back, "Love you too, Dad." She slammed the car door behind her.

From his rearview mirror, he watched as she headed toward Main, losing sight of her after she turned behind Glover. As he parked his car, he thought about flashing into his office to avoid stepping out of his air-conditioned car and into the muggy, humid air. He had even considered convincing Michaela to take the bus in from home, so he could flash to work to save time. Time was becoming increasingly more important to him, constantly thinking about if he had gotten to Olivia before the paramedics, that maybe he could have found a way to save her. Every moment should be utilized, he thought as he stepped out of his car, hoping that his decision to keep his flashing a secret from the world was all worth it.

At the end of the school day, Michaela crept into David's office with her gaze fixed on the floor. She didn't lift her head when he asked about her first day.

"Can we just go home now, please?" David recognized the urgency in her voice, the way she was wrapping her long, brown hair around her hand, and her refusal to make eye contact. These were the telltale signs of her holding back tears, as he had seen too many times over the past nine months. Through countless failed attempts at calming her down, he learned that getting her alone and avoiding conversation and eye contact was the only effective way to let her unwind. He led them through the hallways, walking slightly ahead of her, and out to the car. She threw herself into the front seat, and he started the car. Hushed breaths escaped her as she darted her gaze around to make sure nobody saw her about to break. As he turned the car out of the parking lot and onto the road, out of the sight of anyone involved with Thayer Academy, she whimpered, "I fucking hate this place." Her head flung down into her hands as her back heaved with her wailing cries. David desperately wanted to assure her that everything was going to be okay, to put his arms around her and hold her until the tears stopped streaming, to believe that he could do the job of two parents by himself, but he couldn't. He would remain quiet. She would cry until she was all cried out as she had done before, and only then would she be ready for him to speak. Stopping her midway through her meltdown would only make matters worse. He stole quick glances at her while she bawled into her palms, crumpled into a fetal-like position in the front seat. The sobbing lasted for thirteen of the fifteen minutes it took to commute home before she finally invited him to speak.

"You know what the worst part about today was?" She let the silence hang in the air for a moment, knowing he wasn't going to answer her question.

"Not only did I not fit in with any of the girls here—"

"Hey, now."

"But once my teachers figured out who I was, they looked at me differently. I wasn't just a new kid, I was a new kid they knew everything about. It was like they looked at *me* like I was the dead one, Dad. *Me.* I thought it would be different here. I thought it would be a clean slate where everyone didn't need to tiptoe around me because they felt sorry for me. It's like they think I'm going to lose it at any moment if someone says "mom." Do you know what I mean, Dad?"

As David pulled into their driveway, moments after she finished her rant, he couldn't find any words to comfort her. He was all too familiar with that exact feeling, but had never found the way to describe it. He thought about the day he returned to work after that winter break and how his students uncomfortably looked around at one another. Clearly they all knew about Olivia's death but didn't want to bring it up, didn't want to watch him relive the horrible news, didn't want to remind him in case by some miracle he forgot about it for a moment. How could he blame them? He didn't even know how to address his students, let alone disguise his escapes during the middle of a lecture to the bathroom stall to weep inaudibly. After silencing the engine, stilling the rattling car, he placed his hand on her shoulder, and she collapsed into his chest over the center console. They held each other for a moment, only Michaela's muffled, choked cries filling the car.

For the next few weeks, as Michaela struggled to find her place at Thayer, David began to experiment with his flashing. On the night that marked ten months since Olivia's death, David found himself once again in the basement sifting through the photo albums clustered by the wooden chair. He held a photo album as he flashed to places, discovering that he could carry things with him as he moved freely to new landscapes. Knowing this, he took himself to their first apartment. He stole pinecones from the sidewalk and then flashed to her grave. He placed each pinecone on top of her marble headstone and took a step back to marvel at the engraving. When he bought the plot at the cemetery, it didn't occur to him right away that he would also have to buy a space for himself.

The blank section beneath Olivia's name, the space where his name would eventually go, sent spiders crawling underneath his skin. The thought of his own mortality at forty-seven years old was daunting. Especially after examining the slab, seeing the dash between her birthday and death, David felt defeated. He realized that everything she ever was had been boiled down into a single mark on a block of stone. All of the memories she carried, all of her dreams, and all of her aspirations would go unfulfilled. Sickened by this thought, he took himself to all of their favorite places, flashing through them one after another, taking no time to be in just one place. His vision of all of the places didn't blur into one another, rather they placed themselves on top of each other as if he had laid them all like transparencies onto an overhead projector. Their first apartment, Long Nook Beach, restaurants throughout Boston, the chapel where they got married, all formed into one concrete image. David could essentially be in any number of places at once. After he was full of Olivia induced nostalgia, he landed back at his basement in the wooden chair with the photo albums. Lifting his gaze from the ground, he looked at the clock, noticing that only three minutes had passed. In disbelief, he flashed around again, cycling through places for what seemed to be half an hour. When he finished, the clock hadn't moved. Time stood still when he flashed.

On Thanksgiving, David was reading, sitting alone at the kitchen table waiting for Michaela to get home. The clock was inching closer to 12 AM, nearly an hour after her curfew. She had left saying she was going to a friend's house to watch a movie. He could tell she was lying. Not only was her wavy hair flat ironed straight, a clear sign that she was going somewhere special, but she escaped from the house before he could ask any questions. The front door creaked open. She was slow, yet deliberate to sneak back into the house, probably expecting that David had already gone to bed. From the kitchen, he heard the front steps crack and squeak as she tried to get upstairs to slip into her room unnoticed. Rising from the kitchen table, he called to her as he walked to the front hall. She was almost at the top of the staircase when he saw her, frozen on the second to last step.

"Do you know what time it is?" He questioned.

"I didn't think you would be awake."

"And that makes you coming home this late acceptable?" David felt himself becoming increasingly more aggravated. Staying up until midnight, not knowing where she had been, her attempt at deceiving him were all chipping away at his composure.

"I'm sorry."

"Sorry isn't going to cut it, Michaela. Get down here and tell me what you were doing tonight."

Her descent down the staircase looked pathetic. She clutched onto the handrail as she walked down, looking at her hand more than at David. "Nothing, Dad. Just watching a movie and hanging out. I lost track of time." She reached the bottom of the staircase, standing before David. Strands of her hair fell in front of her face, shielding her eyes from David's glare. A pungent pong floated off of her. David recognized the smell.

"Michaela, were you smoking pot?"

"No!" She retorted.

"You reek."

"Other kids were smoking. It wasn't me."

"Don't you lie to me."

"I'm not! I wasn't smoking, Dad!" As she was losing her temper, she pushed the hair that fell in front of her face behind her shoulders. With nothing blocking her eyes, David could see how bloodshot they really were. Her eyelids looked heavy, slightly tightening her eyes, and her pupils were so dilated he could barely see her green irises.

"Your eyes are as red as tomatoes. If you don't tell me the truth right now, you're going to be in a whole lot of trouble."

Tears started to well in her eyes. "Do you know how fucking hard it is to not have any friends?" Her voice sounded like someone had crammed a plastic bag down her throat. "I'm trying my best to fit in, and I just don't belong here. They're all a bunch of rich, little private school girls. All they do is drugs that they buy with their parent's money. So, yeah, I needed to fit in, Dad. I'm tired of being alone."

David was growing impatient. His words sounded more curt and harsh than he expected, talking louder until he was near screaming: "That doesn't excuse the fact that you smoked. I have so few rules for you, and you go and break two in one night!"

"I'm sorry! What do you want me to say here?"

"There's nothing you can say!"

"You just don't know what it's like!"

"What what is like, Michaela?"

"What it's like to be me!" Rivers of tears were flowing down her cheeks. She was gasping for air between her cries and screams.

"You're not supposed to have your mom die when you're only fourteen!"

"Do you think you're the only person who lost someone here!" He roared. He felt sweat start to pool on his back as his body grew hot with anger. Fear painted Michaela's face, but that didn't stop him from letting all of his frustration out. "It's not just you here! You think it's easier being me! I have to sleep in the same bed without my fucking wife!" With his swearing, Michaela silenced, cowering with her hands in front of her chest. He had never lost his temper, let alone swear around Michaela, and at that moment, she was about to witness all of his pent-up rage, grief, and guilt. "I had to run out in the middle of my lessons to cry in the bathroom! You think being a grown man bawling in a bathroom stall is what you're supposed to do! I still wear this fucking wedding ring because I'm not ready to let go!" He looked down at his wedding ring, still snug around his finger. The veins in his hands and arms bulged out of his body, and he formed fists so tight that his knuckles flared hot white. He launched his fist at the wall hugging the staircase, sending his hand through the sheet rock. When he retrieved his hand, blood streamed down his fist and onto the floor. Michaela gasped. Wrapping her arms around David's chest, she begged for him to stop. Looking down at his hand, then his daughter, his anger subsided, and deep, brooding sadness filled its place. He began to weep, despising himself for losing his composure, for not knowing the right way to deal with grief, and for asking Olivia to go to the store that night to grab champagne rather than driving there himself. It should have been him. This was all his fault. He folded onto the stairs crying into his daughter's arms as she held him.

"It's all my fault. This is all my fault."

"What do you mean, Dad?"

"I asked your Mom to drive to the store that night. It should have been me."

"It's going to be okay, Dad. It's going to be okay."

It took about four weeks for David's hand to fully heal. When the doctors removed the cast, small scars spotted his knuckles. Over the course of that time, Michaela became more reserved, hiding in her room and quickly retreating from family dinners. She continued to go out on weekends, but rather than coming home reeking of smoke, she masked herself in perfume. Sure, David could tell exactly what she was doing. She was covering it up, poorly albeit, but at least making an effort to hide her indiscretions.

On the day after Christmas, they were both overly aware of the impending anniversary of Olivia's death. Michaela came down from her room and joined David at the kitchen table as he graded his students' midterm exams.

"Are there any real bad ones in there?" She asked, flipping through the stack of graded tests.

"So far so good. Only one F, so I'll call that a good year." They both shared a meek laugh. The smile from Michaela's face melted into a flat line.

"I'm worried about Mom's one year anniversary. The monthly reminders are already bad enough."

"I know, I know. I am too," he added. "I've been trying to keep myself busy to get my mind off of it."

"Is that working?"

"Not at all."

He had been flashing to her grave nearly every night of December. The cemetery was eerily peaceful in the winter. The snow blanketed everything, creating a rolling valley of peaks and hills. Small icicles clung onto tree branches that stretched out over the roads reflecting the moonlight. There were a few times where he noticed a freshly plowed section of land, marking that someone else would be joining Olivia in the ground. He wondered about that person, who they were and who they were leaving behind. Perhaps they skidded off of the road because of a patch of ice. Maybe someone had a few too many drinks before getting in the car. And with the next storm, that new plot would be covered again as if nothing had happened, hidden by the banks of snow.

"I'm going to go over Kate's tonight if that's alright with you."

"Yeah, yeah, of course. Just try to be home before curfew please."

"I promise." She got up from her seat and hugged him. He squeezed her, wishing that Olivia could feel that hug somehow.

David was lying on the couch watching TV, waiting for Michaela to come home. The VHS player beneath the TV showed it was only 10:18, at least another half an hour before she would come home. His eyes fluttered, dozing off every few minutes or so then waking back up to the clock creeping toward 11:00. During one of his miniature naps, the lock of the front door thumped open. It was 10:40. She made it home before curfew. Walking into the TV room, her steps looked uneven, slightly wobbling in as if she were only wearing one shoe.

"Hey, Dad. I'm home," she slurred her words ever so slightly, enough to notice but not enough for him to address it. He could have been imagining it, perhaps affected by his drowsiness. After telling him about her night, she headed upstairs and into her room. He followed behind her up the staircase and into the bathroom.

While brushing his teeth, a thud echoed through the halls. He called out to Michaela still with the toothbrush in his mouth. No answer came from her room. Walking toward her room, he asked what the noise was, only to find her body crumpled on the floor. He fell to his knees beside her to shake her body, but she didn't respond. Faint breaths leaked out of her mouth, definitely breathing but in terrible shape. He snatched the phone from her side table and frantically dialed 911.

"My daughter! She collapsed and isn't responding to me. Send someone here now! 15 Carter Street!"

The operator told him they dispatched an ambulance. Putting his fingers on her neck, he searched for a vein, a pulse, anything. The pumps of blood came slowly with too much time in between. Something was severely wrong, and he couldn't wait any longer for the EMT. Taking her in his arms, he flashed to the hospital, abandoning his concern to keep his ability a secret. Appearing at the emergency room doors, he rushed in, her limp body dangling in his arms.

"Somebody help me!" He bellowed. "Someone save my daughter!" Nurses flocked toward him from behind the front desk and hallways. They got her on a gurney and rolled her down the hallway into an open room. A team of doctors and nurses began their work. David paced behind them, trying to peer over their shoulders. All he could hear was the EKG machine mimic her heartbeat, noticing more and more time passing before the next beep echoed through the room.

"Do something!" He thundered. "She's fucking dying!"

"Stand back, sir!" One of the nurses yelled.

Clamping his mouth onto his knuckle, he watched as the team of doctors and nurses hovered over his daughter. They weren't going fast enough, he thought. There was more they could be doing.

"We're losing her!" The doctor shouted. With that cry for help, David pushed the nurses out of the way. He wrapped his arms around her, and flashed faster than he's ever flashed before. Cycling through any possible place he could think of, he took Michaela to hundreds of locations, not even thinking of where they were going. He was too focused on her, staring at her still face. Every day she was looking more and more like Olivia. The crinkle in the center of her nose matched her mother's. The wave of her hair sprawled across her shoulders reminded him of how Olivia would lie on the ground with Michaela as a baby, tugging at her mom's hair. Of course, her eyes were identical to Olivia's—radiantly green as if they were polished emeralds crafted by the finest jeweler. He prayed for her to wake up, to see her eyes open, to hold on to his daughter and what was left of his wife.

David looked up from his daughter at the landscape before him. Nothing about it looked recognizable, nothing like a place he had ever been to. As if he were lost in deep space, all he could see were colors pulsating and churning into one another. This wasn't Long Nook, or Thayer, or even their home in Quincy. His flashing had broken the rules of time and space, transporting him into a vacuum of colors and faraway glints that looked like stars. Their bodies even appeared to be floating, bound by nothing and drifting through vast emptiness. There was no order, no control, just colors colliding and crashing in the distance as if they were trapped in a tumbling kaleidoscope.

As he was trying to make sense of this new space, Michaela's eyes started to flutter open, revealing the shiny emeralds behind her glassy eyes. She looked up at David and beyond him out into this world of tie-dye colors dancing with one another. He was too preoccupied to notice her waking up.

"Dad," Michaela whispered. "What—what is this place?"

He looked down and saw her move. The color rushed back into her cheeks and face. He squeezed his daughter, bringing her head right under his and holding on with all of his might.

"I don't know, but all I care about is that you're alright. I'll never let anything like this happen again. I love you so much, Michaela."

He loosened his grip so he could look at her. Tears were welling in both of their eyes, making the whites of their eyes match the flushness of their cheeks. Circling through this seemingly endless world, this world where they were everywhere and nowhere, released from the grips of time and order, only they existed.

"I love you too, Dad."

63644257R00045

Made in the USA
Middletown, DE
27 August 2019